Praise for Quim Monzó

"Today's best known writer in Catalan. He is also, no exaggeration, one of the world's great short-story writers."
—*The Independent*

"A gifted writer, he draws well on the rich tradition of Spanish surrealism . . . to sustain the lyrical, visionary quality of his imagination."
—*New York Times*

"Monzó blends verve and precision in these stories while also posing bold philosophical questions."
—*Kirkus Reviews*

"Quim Monzó joins contemporary short-story writers such as Etgar Keret and George Saunders . . . to show the absurd in the real, and how the absurd reveals the real."
—*World Literature Today*

"To read *The Enormity of the Tragedy* is to enter a fictional universe created by an author trapped between aversion to and astonishment at the world in which he has found himself. His almost manic humor is underpinned by a frighteningly bleak vision of daily life."
—*Times Literary Supplement*

Other works by Quim Monzó available from Open Letter

Gasoline
Guadalajara
A Thousand Morons

WHY, WHY, WHY?

stories

QUIM MONZÓ

Translated from the Catalan by Peter Bush

Originally published in Catalan as *El perquè de tot plegat* by Quaderns Crema, 1993

First edition, 2019

Library of Congress Cataloging-in-Publication Data: Available.
ISBN-13: 978-1-948830-04-1 | ISBN-10: 1-948830-04-3

This project is supported in part by an award from the National Endowment for the Arts and the New York State Council on the Arts with the support of Governor Andrew M. Cuomo and the New York State Legislature.

The translation of this work has been supported by the Institut Ramon Llull.

LLLL institut ramon llull
Catalan Language and Culture

Printed on acid-free paper in the United States of America.

Text set in FF Scala, a serif typeface designed by Martin Majoor in 1990 for the Vredenburg Music Center in Utrecht, the Netherlands.

Design by Anthony Blake

Open Letter is the University of Rochester's nonprofit, literary translation press:
Dewey Hall 1-219, Box 278968, Rochester, NY 14627

www.openletterbooks.org

Contents

Sir, Jean Giradoux (in *Siegfried et le Limousin*, Chapter 2) raised the interesting question of how, sometimes, minor mysteries in one's life are suddenly belatedly explained. He adds:

> *Je ne désespère pas de voir se résoudre un jour, en Océanie ou à Mexico, quelques autres énigmes de mon passé; un noeud finit toujours par se défaire du simple dégoût d'être un noeud. La seule d'ailleurs qui me préoccupe vraiment est l'énigme Tornielli; cet ambassadeur en exercice, que je voyais pour la première fois à la distribution des prix du concours général, me fit signe d'aller à lui et me glissa dans la main un oeuf dur.*

My intensive research on the Tornielli Enigma has so far yielded only the information that Count Giuseppe Tornielli Brusati di Vergano (1836-1908) was Italian Ambassador in Paris from 1895 to 1908. The obvious unanswered questions are: was Giraudoux actually handed a hardboiled egg by the ambassador of a foreign power? Or did he play on the reader the French trick of disassociating "le narrateur" from "l'auteur." If the former, did Giraudoux die without elucidating the Tornielli Enigma? Or has someone else cleared it up?

I wonder if any of your readers knows the answers.

—Marquis of Tamarón, letter to the editor, published in the *Times Literary Supplement*, 28 January, 1983

WHY,

WHY,

WHY?

HONESTY

THE NURSE PUSHES THE CART CARRYING A TRAY WITH A GLASS of water, a bottle of capsules, a thermometer, and a folder into room 93, says "Good evening," and walks over to the bed of the patient who's lying there with his eyes closed. She gives him a desultory glance, consults the clipboard at the foot of the bed with the details of his medication, takes a capsule from the bottle, and picking up the glass of water, says: "Senyor Rdz, time for your medicine."

Senyor Rdz's eyelids don't flicker. The nurse touches his arm.

"Come on, Senyor Rdz."

Fearing the worst, the nurse holds the patient's wrist to take his pulse. It's non-existent. He is dead.

She returns the capsule to the bottle, slides the cart against the wall, and leaves the room. Then runs to the control desk in that wing of the hospital (D) and tells the head nurse that the patient in room 93 has died.

The head nurse looks at her watch. It's really too bad a patient has died at that moment in time. She's off in a quarter of an hour and is especially keen to leave punctually today because she has finally managed to persuade her best friend's fiancé to meet up with her on the pretext she wants to have a word about her friend. Even though she knows (given what this friend has confided) he's a man who won't stand any nonsense and isn't at all interested in small talk, and so it's a sure-fire thing he's invited her to his place to impale her in next to no time on the top of his table between the candles and plates of spaghetti, if he has indeed cooked spaghetti for dinner, as (her friend told her) he almost always does. She is eagerly anticipating the moment. Yet, if she certifies that the patient in room 93 has died, like it or not, she will have to stay on for a while, even though the next shift has arrived, which starts in a quarter of an hour. The dead generate massive amounts of red tape. And they aren't things that can be sorted in a flash. Which means she'll get to her date late. Of course she could call her friend's fiancé, tell him what's happened, and suggest they meet up later or even on another day. But she knows from experience that it's usually fatal to postpone first dates. That when you postpone a first date for one reason, the next will be postponed for another. And for another and another, until the postponement becomes rather definitive. Besides, it's been a dreadful day, and she desperately wants to leave work, go to his house, and get a piece of action.

If she knew the nurse who'd found the dead patient better, she could tell her to pretend she hadn't noticed. That way, one of the nurses on the later shift would find him and the corresponding head nurse could deal with the ensuing paperwork. It wouldn't matter one iota to the people on the next shift. They will have just started work, and the discovery of a dead man won't ruin their day. She would be freed up and could get to her date on time. But she doesn't enjoy that level of trust with this nurse, who is new; there's even the danger she may be afflicted by that obsession with ethics new people sometimes have. Or if that's not the case, she might remember what she's done and one day use it to her own advantage when it suits her.

The head nurse glances back at her watch. Her stress levels are rising. The hands are moving inexorably toward the moment when she should leave, on her way to a date she does *not* want to miss. What should she do? She must decide quickly, because the nurse who found the dead man is starting to look at her as if she can't understand why she's so quiet, deadpan, and unresponsive. She says she will see to it, and tells the nurse to continue on her rounds.

Nor is she in a position to ask the head nurse on the next shift for a favor. Not because she feels any ethical qualms of conscience but, regrettably, because of a *situation* that is still unresolved, mutual hatred exists that's been there from the day they first met.

If she can't find a way around this, will she be stuck there and have to give up on her date? No way. But anxiety means she can't think straight. Things look bleaker by the second.

At the very worst moment, when her brain is giving up on ever finding a way out, the solution walks in through the door: the new doctor, who hasn't been working in the hospital very long and always has a smile for her, a smile that's at once insinuating and inquisitive. *He* is her lifeline. She'll go over to the young doctor, tell him she has a prior engagement she can't cancel and ask him to do her a favor and take responsibility for the dead patient.

Even though she recognizes that, in exchange, his insinuating smiles will soon become a statement of serious intent. But, hey, does she actually want to yield to that doctor's show of serious intent? She'd never previously given it a moment's thought. Her first reaction would have been no. However, after considering the lay of the land and taking a second look, she thinks, why not? Besides, if she decides she really doesn't like him, she can always say no. One gives favors freely. A favor with a price attached ceases to be a favor.

However, the more she thinks about it, the less she feels like saying no. In fact, she wants to say yes. What's more: she really wants him to come up with a piece of serious intent. She wants it so badly she starts thinking less and less about the man she has that date with later and whom she'd imagined impaling her on his table surrounded by spaghetti.

She walks over, opens her mouth, and tries not to be tongue-tied. The doctor's lips are a knockout. They are moist and firm. She'd like to nibble them there and then. Instead she asks him for *that* favor. The doctor smiles, tells her not to worry, to forget all about it and leave: he'll deal with it. The head nurse walks off down the corridor and before entering the locker room, turns round one last time to check that he was still looking at her; he is, they exchange smiles, and she goes into the locker room. She dresses quickly: it's already ten minutes past when she should have left! She leaves the building. Raises an arm to stop a taxi, has second thoughts, lowers it, and stands rooted to the spot. Then she walks off, looks for a telephone box and, while she calls her friend's fiancé and mutters a rather improbable excuse, she is calculating how long it will take the new doctor to come up with a slice of serious intent, and what she might do to help him on he way, if he seems slow on the uptake.

LOVE

THE ARCHIVIST IS A TALL, HANDSOME WOMAN, WITH STRONG, becoming facial features. She is intelligent, witty, and has what people call character. The soccer player is a tall, handsome man, with strong, becoming facial features. He is intelligent, witty, and has what people call character.

The archivist treats the soccer player with contempt. She's mean and unpleasant toward him. Now and then, when he calls her (he always calls her; she never calls him), even if she has a free day, she'll say meeting up is inconvenient. She makes it clear she has other lovers, so the soccer player doesn't think he has any claim on her. She occasionally gives it some thought (not much, in case she realizes she's on the wrong track) and reaches the conclusion that she treats him with contempt because deep down she loves him a lot and is afraid that, if she doesn't treat him like that, she'd fall into the trap and be as much in love with him as he is with her. Each time the archivist decides they should sleep together, the soccer player is so happy because he can't believe it and weeps tears of joy, as he does with no other woman. Why? He doesn't know, but he believes the contempt with which she treats him isn't the whole picture. In no way is it the decisive factor. He knows that deep down she loves him, and he knows that if she plays hard-to-get it's to avoid falling into the trap, and not be as much as in love with him as he is with her.

The soccer player would prefer the archivist not to treat him with disdain or, at least, less so. Because she would then see, on the one hand, that this isn't the only kind of relationship possible between them and, on the other, that she mustn't be afraid of falling in love with him. Because he'd love a show of tenderness from the archivist, the tenderness she is now afraid to show.

The soccer player sometimes goes out with other women. Because he thinks he can't stand it anymore, because he decides he can't tolerate her treating him like a simpleton anymore, whom she hardly even looks at, whom she sweet-talks at will and then ignores.

But he always comes back. And it's not that the others don't interest him. On the contrary: they are wonderful, intelligent, lovely, considerate girls. But not one of them pleasures him the way she does.

One day (an afternoon, while the archivist is smoking and watching him undress), the soccer player plucks up courage and speaks up. He says she shouldn't be so mean, so prickly, that he loves her so much she mustn't be afraid to show her real feelings. That he won't take advantage of any weakness on her part. That if she is tender (and he knows that she is, and knows she doesn't want to show it) he will love her even more. Angrily, she says who does he think he is to tell her what to do and what not to do; she makes him lie down and slaps him on the face. That afternoon the soccer player enjoys himself more than ever.

However, another day when they meet up, quite unexpectedly, she doesn't look as irritable as usual. That surprises the soccer player. Perhaps she's thought it over and, without saying a word, has started to take notice of him. The next morning she's even tender. The soccer player is overjoyed. She's finally understood she shouldn't be afraid. That showing how she feels deep down won't lead to any hurt. They are in bed. The soccer player is so excited he's overwhelmed by her every gesture and caress. He finds special pleasure in every touch. The tenderness is such he doesn't even want to hump: hugging and repeating that they love each other (as she now tells him all the time) is quite enough.

The archivist will never again treat him with contempt. She is so in love with the soccer player that she tells him in the morning, in the afternoon, and at night. She gives him shirts and books. She always gives him what he wants. She now calls him, more and more, to set up daily meetings. And one evening she suggests living together.

The soccer player looks at her coldly, with glassy eyes. Until quite recently he'd have given his right arm for her to suggest just that.

MARRIED LIFE

Zgdt and Bst (married eight years ago) have to travel to a far-off city to sign some documents. They arrive mid-afternoon. As they can't see to their business until the following morning, they look for a hotel for the night. They're given a room with two single beds, two night tables, a desk (with envelopes and paper on hotel letterhead, in a folder), a chair, and minibar with a television on top. They have dinner, stroll along the river and, when they're back in the hotel, each climbs into a bed and takes out a book.

A few minutes later they hear a couple screwing in the adjacent room. They clearly hear the spring mattress squeaking, the woman moaning, and the man's gentler panting. Zgdt and Bst glance at each other, smile, make jokey remarks, wish each other goodnight, and switch off the lights. Aroused by the screwing he can still hear through the wall, Zgdt thinks about saying something to Bst. Maybe she's got the hots like him. He could go over to her, sit on her bed, joke about their neighbors and, quite casually, caress her hair and face and then her breasts. Bst would very likely join in at once. But what if she doesn't? And pushes his hand away and clicks her tongue or, even worse, tells him: "I don't feel like it"? Years ago he wouldn't have hesitated. He'd have known, just before he switched the light off, whether Bst was up for it, whether the moans from the adjacent room had aroused her or not. But, with the cobwebs of so many years together, nothing is obvious anymore. Zgdt turns on his side and masturbates, as silently as he can.

Ten minutes after he's done, Bst asks him if he's asleep. Zgdt replies that he's not, yet. They've stopped moaning in the adjacent room; now they're conversing quietly and tittering. Bst gets up and goes over to Zdgt's bed. She pulls back the sheets, lies down, and starts caressing his back. Her hand goes from his shoulder to his buttocks. Not having the courage to tell her he's just masturbated, Zdgt says he's not up for it. Bst stops caressing him, there's a brief silence, like an eternity, and she goes back to her bed. He hears her pull up the sheets, get inside, and twist and turn. With every turn, Zdgt's remorse at masturbating without first finding out if Bst wanted to screw grows. Moreover, he feels guilty that he didn't tell her the truth. Is there so little trust between them, are they now such strangers he can't even tell her that? Precisely to show that they aren't such strangers, that there's still a glimmer of trust, that maybe they can re-kindle the fire, he plucks up courage, turns toward her, and confesses that he masturbated a few minutes ago because he thought she wouldn't want to screw. Bst says nothing.

Minutes later, Zgdt imagines, from the surreptitious sounds he can hear, that Bst is masturbating. Zgdt feels hugely sad, thinking that life is absurd and unfair, and bursts into tears.

He cries into his pillow, sinks his face in as far as he can. His tears are hot and plentiful. And when he hears Bst suppressing her final moan with the palm of her hand, he screams a scream that's the scream she is holding back.

SUBMISSION

THE WOMAN EATING VANILLA ICE CREAM AT THE FRONT TABLE IN the café has always been quite candid. She is seeking out (and will do so until she finds him) what she calls a real man, one who is on the ball, who doesn't waste time on gallant pleasantries, on futile frippery. She wants a man who doesn't hang on her every word, say, when they're having dinner. She cannot stand men who try to be understanding and look angelic as they say they want to share the burden of her problems. She wants a man who's not worried about any feelings she might have. From adolescence she has avoided callow youth who spend their time talking to her of love. Of love! She wants a man who never speaks of love, who never says that he loves her. She thinks a dewy-eyed man saying "I love you" is ridiculous. She'll say she loves him (she says it a lot, because she'll really love him), and when she's said it, she'll be delighted by the understanding glance he directs her way. This is the kind of man she wants. A man who will use her in bed the way he wants, without worrying about what she wants, because her pleasure will come from what he gets out of it. Nothing irks her more than the kind of man who, at one moment or another during copulation, enquires whether she has or hasn't achieved an orgasm. On the other hand, he must be intelligent, successful, and lead an intense life of his own. He mustn't be dependent on her. And must like traveling, and have other women apart from herself (and be up-front about it). The latter doesn't worry her one bit, because she knows he only has to whistle and she will be at his feet, ready for whatever he demands, because she wants him to give her orders. She wants a man who tells her what to do, who dominates her. Who (when he feels like it) paws her in public, and wildly. And who, as she's not embarrassed by such things in life, gives her a good wallop without stopping to worry if anyone is watching or not. She also wants him to hit her at home, partly because she likes it (she enjoys being beaten like crazy) and partly because she's convinced that, with everything she has to offer, he could never do without her.

THE MENSTRUAL CYCLE

In the third year of her Biology degree, Grmpf is in love with Pti and Pti with Grmpf. However, as Pti is a tad shy or proud, he never lets on to Grmpf, and Grmpf ends up thinking he isn't in fact in love with her. So she strives to put him out of her mind. It's a battle and a half, because she's very much in love with him, but in the end she manages to half forget him. Particularly from the moment she gets to know Xevi and take an interest in him. Which suits Xevi to a T, because he'd have clung to a red-hot poker: he's just broken up with Mari and feels totally alone. In a rush, like people who want to bury the past as fast as they can, Xevi and Grmpf marry immediately. When Pti finds out, he's completely flummoxed: he realizes at once that he was very, very much in love with Grmpf. He waits by her front door and, the second he sees Xevi leave, he rings the bell. Grmpf opens the door and is astonished to see Pti with one knee on the ground, declaring himself. Her emotions trigger inner turmoil, she's on the point of doubting her actions, but she's strong, takes a deep breath, and tells him it's too late. Pti says nothing, stands up, and walks away, despairing, not wanting her to see his tears. Meanwhile, on the way to the office, Xevi has bumped into Mari. Oh, what a coincidence. They only have to look into each other's eyes to realize that breaking up was a mistake. They hug and pledge eternal love. Though Mari is worried about Xevi: she's not convinced by his quick change of heart, or that he loves her, not Grmpf. Xevi insists he does, that he really loves her, and to prove it he goes back to Grmpf's place when he reckons she won't be there; he packs his suitcase and leaves her a note, saying what has happened and how sorry he is. When Grmpf comes home, she sees the note and feels desperate. How stupid she was not to accept Pti's proposal. She opens a bottle of vodka and drinks every drop. That allows her to pluck up courage. She calls Pti, she tells him she's had second thoughts, and that she loves him.

There's a silence at the other end of the line. Finally, Pti clears his throat and speaks. He says her declaration is rather late because, when she said no, he was so distraught he immediately started a process of denigration, which was so rapid, by that evening he'd destroyed the high opinion he held of her and totally transformed the love he felt for her up till that afternoon. Now he only feels hatred, an intense hatred that allows him to reject her outright and hang up. Phone in hand, Grmpf bursts into tears, and immediately comes down with a fever: she's suddenly 39.2°C. She doesn't go to work the next morning. That afternoon, a friend from the office, Toni, appears, flourishing a bunch of flowers, to see how she is and whether she needs anything. Grmpf is aware that there is a glimmer of love behind his concern and that bouquet. But now is not the time. For now, she can only think of Xevi, until that wound heals.

The wound heals, Grmpf gets over it completely, and Toni persists: he takes her for a stroll, he takes her out to dinner, they go to the movies. He'd like to go further, but she makes it plain from the start that they are going be good friends and nothing more. Toni acquiesces. He acquiesces because he is so understanding. He understands Grmpf's feelings are still raw and can't be toyed with. Every Saturday, on the way back from the movies or a restaurant, he leaves her by her front door and they say goodbye with a kiss on the cheek.

Until one day Toni meets Anni. It's what they call love at first sight. They get involved immediately and Toni stops seeing Grmpf. Grmpf is upset and decides that Toni's not going out with her anymore because all he wanted was to jump into bed with her and, as that didn't happen, he stopped dating her. This is the proof: as she's not an easy woman, he's ended the hypocrisy of their dinners, their moviegoing, and the phrase he liked to repeat: "I'm not worried. I know you're still grieving over Xevi; I'm not at all bothered if we don't sleep together. Really, I'm not." Hypocrite. In revenge, Grmpf goes off to a bar and beds the first guy she meets, a Scotsman by the name of Eric, who's just arrived from Aberdeen and is intending to stay a week, to get a girl by the name of Fiona out of his head.

CLUELESS

THE UNIVERSITY TEACHER GOES TO ANOTHER UNIVERSITY teacher's place for lunch. They must have been working together for a dozen years and now and then (every one or two years) they have lunch together and talk about how things have gone since they last met up. On this occasion it's been almost three years since they last went out to lunch: from before the time she went through a divorce.

She goes on all the time about whether people are a turn-on or not. "Do you think Kim Basinger's a turn-on?" she asks, "I don't think Mickey Rourke is." "Bruce Willis really is." "There's a teacher in my department who's a big turn-on." "Do you think Andreu's a turn-on?"

It's the negative caricature of a certain kind of man talking about women. But the details make it absurd. The men she caricaturizes quite unawares would never ask if such and such a woman was a turn on. They'd know from the first moment they saw them, whether at the movies, in a magazine, or in the department. Nor would they always use "she's a turn-on" as the only phrase in their repertoire; they'd have fifty others, from the poetic to the obscene, to describe each and every one of the anatomical details or lascivious potential they can intuit.

After years and years of devoted married life, she has now (since her divorce) discovered the Mediterranean. However, it's so long since she last swam she's forgotten how to, or swims so tentatively she can only go a few yards out.

She never sits still in her chair. She lights one cigarette after another and sucks them avidly. Her lips are a bright red. She never used lipstick before her divorce. She rarely used makeup either. Now, on the contrary, her face looks like a garish sticker. When she smiles (she smiles all the time) her makeup crumples like cardboard at the corner of her lips. And her hair is a perfect cut, dyed a reddish brown that gives her white strands a coppery-gray hue.

While they drink their coffees, the university teacher listens and watches. Perhaps she's regretting all those years lost to faith in monogamy? Perhaps she's taking a roll call of all the men she wanted to bed and didn't? Perhaps she's just aware that, being so faithful to fidelity, her flesh has gone flabby, she's got wrinkles, and that the people who'd have liked to screw her ten years ago wouldn't be interested now?

"Why are you staring at me so hard?" she suddenly asks. "You're not coming onto me, are you?"

FAITH

"What if you don't love me?"

"But I do."

"How do you know?"

"I don't. I just feel it. Sense it."

"How can you be sure what you *sense* is your love for me and not for someone else?"

"I love you because you're different from all the women I've ever known. I love you like I've loved no one else, as I can never love again. I love you more than I love myself. I'd give my life for you, I'd let myself be skinned alive for you, and let people play with my eyes like they were bullets. Or throw me into a sea of sulfuric acid. I love you. I love every fold of your body. I'm happy just looking into your eyes. I see myself, so tiny, in your pupils."

She shakes her head, nervously. "Oh, Raül, if I only knew that you really loved me, that I could believe you, that you're not lying to yourself and to me as well . . . Do you really love me?"

"Yes, I love you like nobody has ever loved before. I'd love you even if you rejected me, even if you didn't want to see me. I'd love you silently, on the sly. I'd wait for you to leave work just to get a distant glimpse of you. How can you doubt that I love you?"

"How can you expect me not to have doubts? What actual proof do I have that you love me? Sure, you say you love me. But that's words, and words are conventions. I know I love you lots. But how can I be sure that you love me?"

"By looking into my eyes. Can't you read in them how much I really love you? Look into my eyes. Do you think they could lie to you? I'm disappointed in you."

"You're disappointed in me. You can't love me that much if you're so quick to be disappointed. And you ask how can I possibly doubt your love!"

He looks into her eyes and takes her hands in his.

"I love you. Are you listening? I *love* you."

"Oh, 'I love you,' 'I love you' . . . It's so easy to say . . . "

"What do you want me to do? Kill myself to prove it?"

"Don't be so melodramatic. I don't like your tone. You get so impatient so fast. If you really loved me, that wouldn't happen."

"That's not true. I'm only asking one thing: what would convince you that I love you?"

"I'm not the one who has to say it. It has to come from you. Things aren't as easy as you might think."

She pauses. Gazes at Raül and sighs resignedly. "Maybe I should believe you."

"Of course you should!"

"But why? Because you tell me you're not lying, that you really do believe you love me, and that's why you say you do, even though in your heart of hearts, quite unaware, you really don't? You could be wrong. I don't think you mean to be. When you say you love me I think it's because you really think you do. But what if you're wrong? And what you feel for me isn't love, but affection, or something similar? How do you know it's real love?"

"This is upsetting me."

"I'm sorry."

"I only know that I love you, and I find your questions baffling. I'm getting annoyed."

"Maybe because you don't love me."

PYGMALION

She's such a beautiful adolescent that, the moment he meets her, Pygmalion wants to sculpt her. He takes her to his studio and spends hours there (first drawing, then painting her), before making the first clay model. Unlike in the film, the girl isn't an ignoramus and doesn't speak like a deadbeat. By the time he finishes the sculpture they've fallen in love.

In bed, Pygmalion discovers she is as beautiful and well-mannered as she is inexpert. Conscious of his role in the story, he teaches her everything he knows, and is surprised by how quickly she learns. Until he transforms her into the perfect lover, aware that's what she is: the one he'd always dreamt of. She adapts to whatever game he subjects her to, until he's subjected her to every one he knows. Spurred on by the girl's receptivity, he rummages in his hoard of fantasies for some he's never put into practice. Until he's not the only one suggesting ideas, and they both ignite a spiraling crescendo of thrills. Now the girl is at his feet, mouth open, eyes on fire. Holding a spoon, Pygmalion collects the mixture of semen and tears streaming down the girl's face and puts it in her mouth, feeding her like a baby. Pygmalion looks on, enraptured and anxious, as the girl licks the spoon. What else can he do? The girl begs him to do whatever he wants.

"Just say the word and I'll drag myself down the street. If you want, I'll bring men home so you watch them fuck me. Call me 'whore'—that's what you've made me."

It's true. He knows he only has to say the word, and she'll drag herself down the street. But he also knows that, even if he doesn't say the word, she'll do it all the same. You only have to take one look at her. Anyone who looks into her eyes will see she is a volcano of lust. That not only will she never refuse to do anything, she'll grab the first opportunity to be unfaithful, to enjoy the pleasure of deceiving the man who was her teacher. And what if she's already betrayed him and, knowing he'd like to know and find out every detail, she's saying nothing out of pure perversion? It drives him crazy to think another man is fucking her, when he's not present, and he's missing it all. He looks at her at once furious and passionate. He throws the spoon to one side, and stands up; when he looks back at her again, his heart thuds uncontrollably. On an impulse he collects up the few things the girl possesses in his study (hairbrush, earrings, lipstick, a book), stuffs them in a bag, grabs the girl's wrist, sticks it under her armpit, opens the door, throws her out, and slams the door.

"Whore!"

IMMOLATION

Husband and wife gaze at the silhouette of the tower. The wife feels particularly tender and gives her husband a hug.

"I so wanted to do this trip."

They kiss. The husband strokes his wife's hair. They look back at the tower.

"When do we have to be in Florence?" asks the wife.

"Tonight. Are you hungry? Should we get the car and find somewhere for lunch?"

"Yes. But first let's climb the tower."

"The tower? You must be joking."

"Why? Are you saying we've come to Pisa and will leave without climbing the tower?"

"That's right. I, for one, am not going up."

"Why?"

"It's not safe. It wouldn't be much fun if it collapsed just when we're doing the tourist thing and going up."

"Why do you think it's going to fall? It's stayed up like that for centuries. You shouldn't think it'll collapse the moment we climb up."

"Yes, it's been like that for centuries. But it hasn't been leaning that much for centuries. It's been getting worse. And one day it will collapse. Everyone will say: 'You see, it happened today, who'd have thought?' And I don't want to be inside when it does."

"But they had it closed for years, until they made sure nothing was shifting, until a committee of geologists, architects, and God knows who decided there wasn't any danger."

"Exactly. The fact they closed it for years means it *is* dangerous. It won't be a danger once it collapses because then nobody will be able to climb up. The issue is all about before the fall. Besides, they only reinforced the tower with steel rings, anchored it in a cement base, and provided a lead counter-weight. And the fact only a limited number of people can go up at a time is proof they haven't fixed it."

"No. It's proof they've taken the necessary safety measures. Nothing can go wrong now."

"On the contrary. More things can go wrong now than ever before. Before, as time went by, the tower steadied itself. Now all those steel rings and other additions have taken away its relative stability. Now is when it's most likely to fall. Any moment now."

"I don't know what to say. You really don't want to climb up? We're in Pisa, and you're refusing to climb the tower with me?"

"It's an unnecessary risk."

"Everything is an unnecessary risk. Traveling by plane. By car. Smoking. Even staying at home. Maybe a downstairs neighbor hasn't turned off the gas, someone lights a match and the whole building blows up."

"You're being silly."

"I'm going up. Wait here if you want."

There's a strong gust of wind. The scarf the wife is wearing around her neck blows over her face. She pulls it away and scowls at her husband. He realizes that if he refuses it would be the first crack in the wall uniting them, a wall they've been shoring up for years. Because he'd do anything to prevent that wall from cracking, he consents.

"All right, let's go," he says.

She smiles, puts her arm around his waist; they walk toward the tower, begin to climb, and she doesn't even have the time to register this proof of love.

KNOWLEDGE

WHENEVER THE KNOWING WOMAN BEDS SOMEONE, SHE TELLS her boyfriend she did so, not out of a casual attack of lust, but because she has fallen in love. It's not that it amounts to feeling guilty about anything (she and her boyfriend have a very clear, elastic agreement on that front), but it's as if she feels cleaner if, when she beds someone, she observes that she does so for love. Conversely, whenever her boyfriend has a fling with somebody, she thinks he does so simply out of lust, and that irritates her. It's not that she gets jealous. No. She's not jealous at all. She's simply annoyed her boyfriend is so basic, so instinctual. He *does* feel jealous when he knows she's bedding somebody else. But it's jealousy one can understand: because she is in love. And if the person with whom you have a (more or less elastic) agreed *modus vivendi* falls in love with somebody else, then jealousy is the logical outcome.

What scale does the woman apply to determine whether her affairs are a product of love, and her boyfriend's of lasciviousness? He says it's a very simple scale: she is herself (and that justifies everything) and he is not only not her, but is a man, which comes with its own historical baggage. She denies this, though over the years she's learned that, in effect, men and women behave differently. But she doesn't say so, because, even if it's a belief she doubts less and less as time goes by, it is a generalization. And there are always exceptions, although she's never ever been so close to recognizing that the cliché about men being all the same, though commonplace (and therefore repugnant), is true, if only in part: maybe not all, but the vast majority of men are the same. The knowing woman knows what she's talking about: she's fallen in love with lots of men, and every single one, unfailingly, whatever display they put on, date her because they are driven by lust. Lust to which she often yields because (she has to recognize this) she's been loving by nature from a very early age and love is so intoxicating that, as soon as a man puts an arm around her shoulder, kisses an ear lobe, and slides his hand between her legs, though she opens her mouth to say no, she never does, and always says yes.

THE DECISION

THE FEMME FATALE AND THE IRRESISTIBLE MAN MEET IN THE evening in a café with ocher colored walls. They look into each other's eyes: they know this will be the last time. For weeks both have been aware of the evident fragility of the thread that has joined them for three years, that made them constantly call and live for each other; an edginess that meant not even Sunday afternoons were boring. Now the thread is about to break. The moment has come to question their love and then conclude it.

They used see each other every day, and the days they didn't, they'd call, even if it was in the middle of a conference in Nova Scotia. They have barely met three times in recent weeks and they weren't happy encounters. They haven't said as much, but both know today's encounter is to say goodbye irrevocably. They've reached such a state of interpenetration that neither needs to say they are bored because both feel that simultaneously. They hold hands and recall (singly and silently) the fornicating perfection they've recently achieved: they themselves wonder at it. It is hardly strange if, compared to such acrobatics, the rest of their lives must seem insipid. They drink coffee, say goodbye, and go their own ways. She has a dinner date with a man; he has a dinner date with a woman.

After dessert, the femme fatale takes ninety minutes to get into bed with the man she had the date with. The irresistible man takes one hundred and eighty to get into bed with his companion. They both do it so clumsily they are taken aback. How passive! How awkward! How impatient! They have a long, long way to travel before they reach with their new lovers the perfection they just said goodbye to, over a cup of coffee.

ADMIRATION

THE GIRL LISTENS OPEN-MOUTHED AS THE ABSTRUSE NOVELIST reads a chapter from his latest novel. When he finishes, while people clap she grasps her chance to position herself strategically and, when the novelist leaves the room, chatting to this person and that, and shaking the occasional hand, she accosts him. She tells him she is very interested in what he does and, if at all possible, she'd like to get to know him much better. The girl is pretty and the novelist likes pretty girls. He looks at her, she looks into his eyes and smiles. The novelist agrees; he sees off the organizers and they go to a restaurant for dinner.

It's a cheap restaurant, because although he is a good novelist (or precisely because that is what he is) he isn't successful enough to frequent top-notch restaurants. She couldn't care less. She (she realizes when he looks into her eyes) is totally besotted with him. He chatters nonstop, and she likes what he says. She laughs lots and they leave the restaurant in deep embrace. They go to his place, he lives in a top-floor apartment with no elevator ("just like in the movies!" she enthuses) and they spend the night there. They meet again the following day.

They end up moving in together. She's pregnant within four months. They have a baby girl. The apartment becomes not only too small, but too uncomfortable to raise a child there. One evening the abstruse novelist makes a decision: whatever it takes, he must increase his income. Abstruse novels struggle to bring in anything. And what he earns with his commentaries on chess games in the daily paper and what she earns as an assistant in a perfumery, is a total pittance.

Luckily, a friend (who published a couple of books of poetry years ago and now produces ads) finds him a job in an advertising agency. He joins as a copywriter. He's never lacked wit, and knows plenty about writing. So much so, the management recognizes his worth immediately. Things improve, economically and professionally.

Finally they can move to another flat. She's pregnant again. From time to time he recalls the days when he wrote abstruse novels. They are ever more distant. That's a phase that's over and done with, and he sometimes thinks he can't possibly ever have been a writer of abstruse novels. He wouldn't go back to that under any circumstance. He now thinks literature is a moth-eaten thing, an art belonging to centuries past. The future and the present are not in books, which nobody reads anymore, but in daily papers, television, and radio. And advertising, which consciously prostitutes itself, is the art *par excellence*. And he is making it in this art *par excellence*. To such an extent that three years later he is running his own agency, and gets home worn out every day, with time just to give the two girls a kiss before he stretches out on the sofa, grunts, and tells his wife, at machine-gun rate, about his day's thousand and one tasks.

She looks at him pitifully. She knows he doesn't miss the time when he wrote abstruse novels. She knows he struggles daily from dawn to dusk to keep the household afloat, that he does so with good grace and that, what's more, he's a success, and that makes him happy. Sure he wouldn't understand why she pities him, but that is how it is. That's why when they go to bed and he falls asleep immediately, she continues with the light on, reading a novel. It's an intricately plotted novel (it's the new trend; abstruse novels are no longer in vogue) that came out a fortnight ago and has already been successful, a huge success within the residual world of literature. She finds it fascinating, so much so, she doesn't intend to miss the lecture the novelist is going to give in a prestigious cultural institute in the city tomorrow afternoon.

WHY DO THE HANDS OF A CLOCK TURN THE WAY THE HANDS OF A CLOCK DO?

THE BLUE MAN IS IN THE CAFÉ, STIRRING A SPOON IN HIS CUP OF pennyroyal. A magenta man approaches him rather uneasily.

"I need to talk to you. Can I sit down?"

"Please."

"I don't know where to begin."

"At the beginning."

"Last month I seduced your wife."

"My wife?"

"Yes."

The blue man takes a few seconds to respond.

"Why are you telling me?"

"Because I've been miserable ever since."

"Why? Do you love her so much that you want to live with her? Does she not love you and that's what upsets you?"

"No."

"Maybe it's remorse?"

"No. The fact is she won't leave me alone. She calls me night and day. And if I don't answer, she comes to my place. And if I'm not there, she looks for me everywhere. She comes to see me at work, she says she can't live without me."

"And?"

"I've lost my peace of mind. Ever since I met her, I can't get her out of my hair for a single day. Haven't you noticed anything?"

"When did you first meet her?"

"A month and a half ago. You were in Rome."

The blue man was indeed in Rome a month and a half ago.

"How do you know I was in Rome?"

"Don't you believe me? She told me, the day I met her. I met her at a computer class."

The wife had indeed gone to a computer class, taking advantage of the fact the blue man was in Rome.

"So what do you want?"

"For you to help me get out of this. It's not that I don't like your wife. She's fantastic, intelligent, and sensual. What else can I say? But . . ."

"She is very overpowering."

"Isn't she just?" says the magenta man gleefully, seeing that the blue man understands him.

"You want to get her off your back?"

"Yes, in a nutshell."

"She won't leave you alone for a second, right? If she sees you by yourself, smoking, enjoying the fresh air, reading the paper, studying, watching your favorite TV show, whatever, she immediately lies down on top of you and starts buttering you up."

"What's more, if you're not 100 percent into it she thinks she's in the way and gets dramatic that way she does. That's why, though I've no right to, I'd like to ask you a favor: talk to her, be jealous, threaten her. Whatever it takes. Anything to make sure we don't see each other ever again."

"Do you really want to get her off your back?"

"Yes, please."

"Nothing could be easier. Do what I do. Stop avoiding her, don't hide, be nice, warm-hearted, and considerate. Be more into her than she is into you. Call her, tell her you love her like nobody has ever loved before. Tell her you'll devote your whole life to her. Marry her."

JEALOUSY

TAMAR LICKS IT AGAIN AND LOOKS UP VERY SLOWLY UNTIL HER eyes meet Onan's.

"I really like your cock."

She's exhausted. She shuts her eyelids. In next to no time she has dozed off, her head on the pubis of the man who can't stop thinking about what she just said. "I really like your cock." "I really like your cock . . ." Why does she always say the same thing? Ever since they started dating, how often has she said that, when they're lying in bed? Countless times. Conversely, she never says she really likes his right arm or his shoulder blades. It's always: your cock. Sometimes, Tamar holds it in the palm of her hand and it comes out differently: "You've got a lovely cock."

Now she's asleep and the man has turned on his side. To do so, he's had to move her head off. Even though she's dozing, she still clings to it. She is *so* infatuated with his tool. Is his tool all she likes about him? Does she like him? She never says she likes him. Initially, he found her single-mindedness delightful. It was tender and stimulating. Like when he told her: "I really like being inside your cunt." But it gradually became a tad obsessive. It is true that she really does like his cock. He sees that in her eyes, in the way she looks at it, in the rhythm of her words, in the way she emphasizes the word "really": "rreeeally."

He's woken up the next morning by Tamar's mouth caressing it. Onan moves away, as if hurt.

"What are you doing?"

"I really like it."

"You really like it?"

"Yes." She pauses for a second. "I really like your cock."

They're back to that.

"Would you love me as much if I didn't have a cock?"

She looks at him askance.

"What's up with you?'

"What do you think? All you ever talk about is cocks."

"*Your* cock."

"You never say that you like me."

He abruptly removes her hand. Tamar gets up. She is lovely, and indignant.

"You're crazy."

"No, I'm not crazy. But I do exist too." And he adds cuttingly, deliberately so it sounds ridiculous: "Wouldn't you agree?"

Tamar hurriedly gets dressed. She slams the door behind her. Her footsteps echo down the stairs, ever more distantly. Onan sits in bed, puts his right hand on his flaccid member, lifts it slightly and scrutinizes it, half in fury, half intrigued.

HAND ON HEART

THEY GET ENGAGED ON NEW YEAR'S EVE, AT THE STROKE OF midnight, when fireworks erupt across the city and people hug: in homes, in the street, and in dance halls. The era of friendship is at an end for both of them with a betrothal that will lead to marriage. When will they marry? They'll decide later: they're too excited for now. They look into each other's eyes and pledge eternal love and fidelity. They decide to ditch the more or less amorous affairs each had had to this point. They also promise to be totally honest with each other; they will never lie.

"We'll be completely honest. We'll never lie to each other, no way, no excuses."

"A single lie would be the death of our love."

These pledges excite them even more. At two in the morning they fall asleep on the sofa, tired and in each other's arms.

They get up at midday, hungover. They shower, dress, and go out wearing sunglasses.

"Shall we go get lunch?" he asks.

"Yes. A light one, I'd say. A couple of tapas would be fine for me. But you must be ravenous."

He's about to say he's not, that anything would be fine, but he remembers their pledge.

"Yes, I am. But I'd be happy with a few tapas. You eat a couple and I'll eat more."

"No, you must want a real sit-down meal. Wouldn't you rather go to a restaurant?"

They have promised to be totally honest with each other. So he can't say what he would have said if they hadn't: that he's fine with tapas at a bar. Now he must acknowledge that he really would prefer to go to a restaurant and have a sit-down meal.

"Let's do that then," says she. "Let's go to that Japanese restaurant we went to a week ago and that you liked so much."

The previous week they'd not yet promised to be totally honest with each other. Besides, he never told her he had liked the Japanese restaurant. He recalls that clearly: when she asked, he'd said he thought the restaurant was OK, a formula that didn't convey the enthusiasm she is now putting in his mouth.

"I told you I thought it was okay, not that I'd liked it."

"In other words, you didn't like it."

He has to tell her: "I hate Japanese food."

She looks him in the eyes, peeved.

"You know I like Japanese a lot."

"I know."

He wonders if their pledge requires him to do this or not, but, preferring to err on the side of excess rather than commit a sin of omission, he tells her everything else he is thinking: that one of the things he doesn't like about her is precisely (and it ties in with an attitude of hers she thinks is sophisticated, but is basically merely pretentious) her fondness for restaurants that have replaced good cooking with public relations. She tells him he is an idiot. He is forced to say he doesn't feel at all idiotic and that he is convinced, that if they were to test which of them had the most powerful brain, hers wouldn't win out. Such words offend her, and she slaps him, in a rage repeating that he is an idiot, an outright idiot, and will be for the whole of his life, and that she never ever wants to see him again, a sentiment he immediately espouses.

INSTABILITY

Fed up with thieves wrenching out his car radio time after time, Sr Trujillo had one installed that you could remove and put back. That way they'd never steal his again.

He drove out of the repair shop, listening to a program. It was a good radio. When he reached home and parked in the community lot, he'd always take out the radio, stick it under his arm, and go up to his apartment. When he went to the office, he'd do likewise. So, all in all, he carried the radio under his arm for a very short while. From the community lot to home, from the office lot to the office: in each case, short walks plus an elevator ride. That's why it was a hardly a pain to carry it. If he'd had to carry it along the street, he'd have thought differently. He'd always felt contempt for people who walked everywhere with their car radio under their arm. They made him fume, when he saw them at the bar, with the radio beside their glass. Or in shops, dragging it from counter to counter, never losing sight of it, even though the shop assistant concealed it under fifteen shirts.

That's why, a week and a half later, he suddenly stopped in the middle of the street and surveyed his armpit. What was he doing with a radio under his arm? How come he hadn't noticed until he was fifteen yards from his car? He'd driven to the city center to do some shopping and, after spending an exasperating amount of time driving around looking for a parking space, when he'd finally found one, he'd automatically taken the radio out. The tension that had built up as he circled about had caused his brain autonomously (for a moment) to decide that his reluctance as regards carrying his radio down the street under his arm was nonsense. That's why it had taken him fifteen yards to realize. He felt ridiculous. He turned back, opened the car door, and sat down holding his radio. Where could he leave it? Under the seat? Would a potential thief perhaps see it through the rear window? In the glove compartment? He looked down the street to see whether anyone was looking. Nobody was. He opened the glove compartment, put the radio inside, and closed it. Then he got out. He checked that the door was properly shut and headed to the first shop, where he bought some green shoes.

When he came back to his car forty-five minutes later, he discovered that the left window had been broken and his radio stolen.

He went back to the repair shop the next morning. He asked them to fit a new window and another radio. He went to pick up the car that afternoon and drove home full of doubts. What would he do from now on? If he only had to go home or to the office, it wasn't a problem: he would pop in the radio and, once he'd arrived, he'd take it out and carry it up to his flat or office.

However, if he went anywhere else (shopping or a restaurant), he wouldn't leave it in the car, because if he did, it would be stolen.

That's why the following night he drove without his radio. Something he hated doing; he really liked listening to music when he was driving. I mean, why had he had a radio installed if in the end he had to leave it at home? He decided that, until he'd solved that dilemma, he'd leave the car in the lot and travel by taxi.

It was precisely in a taxi, five days later, that he concluded it was foolish to spend a fortune every day on taxis while his car gathered dust in the lot. He thought about selling the car. But soon dismissed the idea: it was generated by indignation and was consequently OTT. There must be a solution that perhaps his nerves were blocking out. For the moment, he would take one step: as he was reluctant to take a taxi when his car was in the lot (so as not to take his car without the radio, or with the radio and then have to carry it around), he'd stay at home and not go out. Besides, if he really must, he could always walk to the bar, the shop, the restaurant, or wherever he wanted to go. However, this decision seriously limited his field of action—unless he was ready to spend three hours getting somewhere and three hours getting back.

On the eighth day of staying in at night, he felt so bored he extracted the TV from the junk room, where he'd put it weeks before, when he started dating that girl who reckoned it was trendy again not to watch television. He dusted it. He plugged it in. They were showing a movie with Jean-Louis Trintignant. After a quarter of an hour the screen turned magenta. He switched it off. He unplugged it and put it back in the junk room. He grabbed his jacket, went out, walked to an emporium three streets away, and bought a new television (a huge one with a rectangular screen); he came home with the technician, connected it, and looked for the channel that was showing the Jean-Louis Trintignant movie.

When the movie finished, it was followed by a made-for-TV movie whose main character was the son of a policeman who, without his father realizing, was helping him solve his cases. Then, the news. Then, a word-guessing competition. In order to participate, you had to send in a label from a well-known canned vegetable company inside an envelope with your name, address, and telephone number. They would select one envelope from the pile. If it was yours, they called you and you had to answer one simple question (live). If you got the right answer, you could participate in the game and try to guess, letter by letter, the word made by the blank squares on the panel. Every square carried a letter and a photo. The photos: different amounts of money, an apartment on the coast, a set of home appliances, a temple in Bangkok, a video camera, a bicycle, a car, and a beach in the Caribbean. Each one indicated the prize won. The simpler the letter, the lower the prize. The trickier the letter, the more valuable the prize. If a competitor opted for easy vowels or consonants, he'd win very little. If you tried to win the big prizes, it involved more unusual letters, and you probably wouldn't get them and you wouldn't complete the word, meaning you wouldn't win any prize at all.

The next morning he bought a can of vegetables of the requisite brand, removed the label, and sent it off. A week later, he watched as they selected his letter. They called him immediately. They asked him the simplest question. Which of the following products didn't the sponsoring firm can?: peas, green beans, tuna, or carrots? He chose the correct answer: tuna. They went on to the panel with the mystery word. Sr Trujillo said the letters. He completed the word: "instability." The "A" won him bundles of twenty-five thousand pesetas. The "T"s, bundles of a hundred thousand. The "S", a television with teletext, and the "N", an apartment on the coast.

The apartment was in a three-story building with a communal garden. The neighbor downstairs was a bald Dutchman who spent the day tending his flowers, one of those retired Northerners who decide to spend the last years of their lives in a cheap, warm country, where retirement money goes a lot further. The upstairs neighbors were a couple. He often met them on the stairs, or heard them moving about in their place. They arrived on Saturday morning and left on Sunday evening. Sr Trujillo went every weekend. He left the city on Friday evening (in his car, with the radio installed) and returned on Sunday at dusk.

One Saturday, the upstairs neighbors invited him to dinner. He accepted. She was Raquel. He, Bplzznt. They dined on avocado and shrimp cocktail and roast beef with gravy. They drank two bottles of wine. They put on some music. The couple danced. Afterward, while Bplzznt poured their whiskeys, Raquel, all smiles, forced Sr Trujillo to dance with her. He was aroused by being cheek to cheek. When the song was finished, he sat on the sofa. So did the couple. They told him about their line of work and how long they'd been married. They wanted to have lots of children. Sr Trujillo left at 1 A.M. He went to sleep, listening to the couple chatting a good long time.

At midday the next morning somebody knocked on his door. It was Raquel and Bplzznt, who were going to the beach. They invited him to join them. As he had nothing else to do, he agreed. They went to a cove that Raquel and Bplzznt knew, out of the way, with three big, equidistant rocks in the water. Nobody else was on the beach. They stretched out on their towels. The couple went for a swim. They swam out to one of the rocks, some hundred yards away. Sr Trujillo dozed off. He was woken up by shouting. He stood up. A few yards from the rock, Raquel was waving her arms, calling for help. Sr Trujillo jumped into the sea. He was hardly a strong swimmer. When he reached her, he felt exhausted, but he joined in Raquel's efforts to search for Bplzznt. To no avail. On the way back to the beach, Raquel sobbed as she told him that Bplzznt had started swimming toward the other rock and, halfway, had started to call for help. Cramps, no doubt.

The police found the corpse after a few hours. He was buried two days later. His wife didn't return to the apartment for three weekends. On the fourth, she did. When Sr Trujillo heard footsteps overhead, he went up. The woman threw herself into his arms and burst into tears. He was aroused by being cheek-to-cheek. He stroked her hair to console her and they started to kiss. They sat on the sofa holding hands. Now and then, one, then the other, removed a hand, picked up a handkerchief, and wiped the tears away. They decided on marriage that same night. They married the following Friday. Once married, they decided to sell one of the apartments. They sold Sr Trujillo's, because if they sold Raquel's and went to live in Sr Trujillo's, their new upstairs neighbors might prove to be very noisy. With the money they made, they refurbished Sr Trujillo's apartment in the city. Two years later they had a baby boy. They named him Bplzznt, in memory of her dead husband. A year later they had a baby girl. The ideal pair! They named her Clara, after Sr Trujillo's mother. Their third child (two years later) was also a girl. They named her Chachacha.

Every weekday morning, before going to the office, Sr Trujillo grabs his briefcase and the boy with one hand and the girls with the other and takes them to school. Bplzznt is now six, Clara, five, and Chachacha, three. First he leaves the boy at the middle school, then the elder girl at elementary school, and the youngster at kindergarten. Then Sr Trujillo walks down the stairs, greets the odd father or mother he meets on the way, ruffles the hair of a boy he knows, and goes back to their block. He gets into his car, takes the radio from his briefcase: he purchased the briefcase so he could conceal the radio inside when he walks his children to school. He inserts the radio, switches it on, tunes in to a program, puts his hands over his face, and, with all the strength he can muster, tries to cry, but the tears never come.

ST. VALENTINE'S

THE MAN WHO NEVER FALLS IN LOVE LEAVES THE MUSEUM AND sits down on a bench in the square opposite. When he was looking at a Manolo Hugué drawing in the museum he met a woman with deep, sparkling, slightly mischievous eyes, and thought that maybe he could fall in love with her. He also thinks that it isn't just her sparkling, slightly mischievous eyes he likes about her. It's also the way she speaks. The whole time they spoke in the museum, she didn't utter a single cliché or parrot any received wisdom she'd learned by heart. That's why, after they said goodbye, he followed her at a distance, until he saw her go into a building entrance; now he's waiting.

From a very early age, the man who never falls in love had intuited that it wouldn't be easy to find the woman of his dreams. As a baby he looked at his babysitter's white socks and legs, and something inside him said it was going to be a rough ride. Especially because he didn't have a clear idea what the woman of his dreams should be like, or, (in fact) whether there would be one. He had no preferences. He didn't imagine her small or tall, blonde or brunette. Nor was he worried about her being especially intelligent, or simple-minded, as some preferred. At the age of five he fell in love with the daughter of the owners of the stationery store near home, where he bought pencils, erasers, pens, nibs, ink, and spiral notebooks. Naturally, he never told her. It was a secret love that kept him awake at night, tossing and turning in his bed, with the image of the bookseller's daughter in his mind's eye: those sparkling, slightly mischievous eyes. Even now, when he thinks of the woman he could fall in love with, he thinks of those sparkling, slightly mischievous eyes. One day, however, her parents sold their store, left the city, and he never heard of her again. He longed for her. To the point that he felt ever more regretful that all he knew about her was that she'd lived opposite and he'd never dared declare himself. He didn't fall in love again until he was eight. He didn't know this at the time, but it would be the last time he fell in love. He fell in love with his big sister's friend, who often came to their house to play. He felt guilty about falling in love with her: it seemed like a betrayal of the stationery-store owner's daughter. His sister's friend must have been twelve and he, a mere eight-year-old, would get nowhere with her. Maybe when he grew up and the distances that now seemed unbridgeable became more relative . . . Then the years went by at a hundred miles an hour, ever more quickly. He's nineteen now. He came of age a year ago. One more year and he would be twenty. Twenty! He'd never have thought he'd get that far, between the ages of twelve and fourteen he'd had this mystical intuition he would die before he reached twenty: in a car or motorbike accident, or else by committing suicide. His worry is: will he never fall in love again? He hasn't been in love with anyone for ten years and is beginning to long for those sleepless nights, tossing and turning in bed, with his beloved in his mind's eye. Maybe that's what becoming an adult is all about. At the end of the day, he ruminates, falling in love is a symptom of immaturity, a sign that one isn't sufficiently independent. What he can't understand is how he can miss something that is rationally so harmful. Why does he feel so empty? Why didn't he fall in love with Marta, the girl he met in his drawing class? She had many good qualities. And defects. But defects you can forgive. Like all defects: indeed, all defects can be forgiven. That was what he thought when he decided to break up with her. But why forgive Marta's and anyone else's? If you have to love someone, if loving really means what it's supposed to, petty defects shouldn't irritate you. And Marta's defects do irritate him. She is presumptuous and obsessive. Obviously she is warm, understanding, and welcoming. But Neus is also warm, understanding and welcoming. Neus, on the other hand, has the drawback that she is too banal, that she's never had an original thought. That drawback is complemented by her aggressive attitude (because she is insecure). A kind of aggression that is typical of people who go clubbing and are quick, as the music blasts away, to show that they are *interesting*. They manufacture the image of being *interesting* through acerbic, pre-fabricated phrases, which can be easily inserted at any point in the conversation. And what about Tessa? Tessa is intelligent, witty, and amusing. And they interpenetrate. They only have to glance at each other across a restaurant table to know, without saying a word, from the glint in their eyes, what they are thinking, who they find boring. What's more, they get on wonderfully well in bed. Conversely, she is a spoiled child, who puckers her lips when she's refused some whim. Moreover, she is lethargic and spends the day supine on the sofa, languidly smoking a never-ending cigarette. Quite unlike Anna, who is always doing something. She is a dynamo who inspires a desire to live. But what is Anna's defect? That she is possessive like no other woman he has ever known, and in the months they dated controlled him day and night, and was always doubting he loved her as much as she loved him. Which was true. Because he never managed to love her however hard he tried. He's fond of her, appreciates her . . . But love, as in true love . . . And it's not as if he is chasing an unattainable ideal. He's not so idiotic as to think he'll find someone without defects. If you really love someone, their defects are consigned to a drawer and not a constant sore point. He tried to love her. Just as he tried to love Tessa, Neus, and Marta. He'd give up his life to be in love with any of them. Because it would be worthwhile falling in love with any of them; if it weren't for that fact that, however hard he tries, he never succeeds. Why can't he be like everyone else and fall in love? Sefa (another girl worthy of arousing love in anyone with a bit of nous) says it surely goes back to a childhood trauma. That neither his mother nor his father had shown him enough love and that is why he is as he is. Another original explanation is the one expressed by Cuqui, who told him on their last day together, before their final goodbye, that his problem is that he can't love anyone because he only loves himself. Because he is an egotist unworthy of the love of the women who fall in love with him. What a great conclusion, if only it were true! And that is another side to it: lots of women fall in love with him. He can't understand that. Why do they all fall in love with him with such frenzied passion? Why is he incapable of falling in love with any of them and properly requiting their feelings?

While he is deep in such thoughts, the man who never falls in love watches as the girl he met in the museum emerges from the building entrance and turns down a street. He springs to his feet. He follows her. Gradually the distance between them shortens. The more he looks at her walking in front of him, the more he likes her, and from what he grasped in the museum, she likes him too. And what if it really went well this time? Now he is a few steps behind her; she's with hand's reach. He'd only have to tap her on the shoulder and she'd turn around.

TROJAN EUPHORIA

THE MAN WHO'D EXPERIENCED A DEGREE OF RELIGIOUS FAITH AS A child is no sluggard. He quickly slips out of the sheets, stretches, jumps up, and runs into the hallway to the bathroom, raising his knees very high like a soccer player in training. He shaves. The smell of his aftershave reinforces his faith in life. He dresses, closes his apartment door, walks whistling into the lift, alights on the ground floor, dodges people in the street, and enters the subway station close to home. He sticks his card in the slot at one end of the barrier, picks it up from the other, and walks through; as he goes down the stairs he hears a train leave and a crowd floods up both escalators and the stairs. He uses the time on the platform to look at movie posters. The next train arrives. Its doors open, he goes in, clings to a pole, and contemplates the face of a man whose eyelids are swollen shut. He looks away and stares at a kid who is observing him very intently.

The man who had experienced a degree of religious faith as a child smiles at the kid. The kid sticks his tongue out. The man, who'd been interested in mathematics as a child, as well as enjoying a degree of religious faith, laughs. An inspector approaches, asking to see tickets. The man who'd been interested in mathematics as a child is amazed that inspectors still exist. He hasn't seen one for years. That's what he's thinking as he rummages in his pockets, looking for the ticket that he had endorsed. He can't find it. It's not in his inside jacket pocket (which is where it should be) or in the outside ones, or in his pants' pockets. It's nowhere; the inspector loses patience.

The man who'd been interested both in mathematics and religion takes out his wallet and opens it, though he doesn't remember putting it there. Indeed, it isn't there. He must have lost it. That's what he tells the inspector: "I must have lost it." The inspector fines him. The man who, as well as taking an interest in religion and mathematics, also had had problems socializing as a child, pays the fine, leaves the subway, and goes up to his office. He takes off his jacket and sits at his desk, still thinking about the inspector and the (pleasant) feeling of nostalgia he felt when he saw they still existed. He looks at the pile of folders heaped in front of him. He opens the first and settles down to work.

Eight hours later he looks up, stands, puts on his jacket, leaves the building, and returns to the subway. He arrives home; his young son runs to welcome him, crying. He hugs his waist. Their dog has died; tears flood down the kid's cheeks. The man who had problems socializing as a child, bends down, hugs his son, and tries to console him. He tells him the dog was very old, that they will buy another, as nice as the one that's died. When his daughter gets back from her English class, he tries to break the news to her as gently as possible. When both children are in bed and he and his wife sit on the sofa in front of the TV, he takes her hand and says that these little upsets are what turn children into adults.

The wife drinks a double gin. The man who, as well as his problems socializing in his youth, owned a leather blouson he still remembers, feels like going out for a drink when he sees his wife downing a double gin. He suggests contacting their babysitter and going out together. His wife refills her glass with gin and tells him to go out if he wants; she doesn't want to.

So he does. He goes to his usual bar. He stays two hours, drinking, talking, and flirting. He leaves at closing time. A female acquaintance leaves right when he does. The man who once owned a leather blouson that he still remembers asks whether he can give her a lift. She says no because she has her own car. Both get in their cars and drive off. A couple of streets later they meet at the same red traffic light, side by side. They look at each other. They smile. The light turns to green. They move off. They meet up at every red light and smile.

The man who in his youth owned a leather blouson he still remembers looks at the woman all dewy-eyed. It's a technique, he says, that gives a good return. But at one of the red lights he yawns when he's looking at her, doesn't brake properly, and hits the car in front, whose driver jumps out, gesticulating angrily.

The man who, in his youth, as well as having a leather blouson he still remembers, and went to Majorca on an end-of-high-school jamboree, also gets out of his car, with a conciliatory smile on his lips, as he watches the woman drive into the distance, laughing and waving goodbye.

The collision wasn't a big deal. The cars have a few dents and nothing more. It could have been worse. They fill in the insurance company forms and exchange names and phone numbers. The next morning, the man who had gone to Majorca on an end-of-high-school jamboree is quick to take his car to the garage. It's only a week till the holidays and it must be ready for then. They tell him to pick it up in two days' time. He rings the mechanic two days later to see if it's ready. The mechanic says he needs to speak to him personally. He should drop by. He drops by: the garage has burnt down and the three cars inside were incinerated. His was one of the three.

He leaves the garage in a state. He thinks about renting a car for the holidays. But his wife doesn't agree: she thinks it will bring bad luck. Her heart tells her that if they rent a car, they will have a fatal accident. But she also says they'll have one if they travel by air, train, or bus. The man who went on an end-of-high-school jamboree to Majorca is quite skeptical about his wife's premonitions, but doesn't feel like arguing. They decide not to go on holiday that year, in order to sidestep the premonitions. Shut up in their flat for two months with the two kids becomes highly claustrophobic; the tensions that have existed between the parents for some time explode. Suddenly everything is a bother; they argue over the slightest thing. They rage. One day, she raises her hand and slaps him. He returns the slap. They immediately calm down. They agree they cannot continue like that. They decide to separate.

They separate at the beginning of autumn. He packs his bags and goes to a (small) apartment that he's rented. He furnishes it straightaway. He takes out a loan for the sofa, television, VCR player, fridge, tables, chairs, and beds. He is happy: he got the car (that the insurance company people have said isn't a total write-off and can be fixed). The man who, as well as going on an end-of-high-school jamboree to Majorca, as an adolescent tried on his mother's bra in front of the wardrobe mirror, can't get over the success of their separation. He's astonished that (though all the evidence is to the contrary) the dismal human custom of coupling and cohabiting has survived over the centuries.

He's thinking all that as he walks up the stairs in a big department store where he has gone to buy clothes. He meets a frankly attractive girl in the shirt section. They immediately feel drawn to each other. Three hours later, in a cafeteria on the Diagonal, the man who as an adolescent tried on his mother's bras invites her to his place. They go. The girl offers to pour out the whiskeys. They screw. It's a quickie. The man reckons it wasn't a particularly wonderful screw. But we know the first often isn't what you'd call great; that's why one must leave the door open to hope. He dozes off. When he wakes up, the next morning around eleven, his place is empty: they've stolen (she couldn't have done all that by herself) his money, credit cards, television, VCR player, sofa, chairs, tables, fridge, even his bottles of whiskey.

A week later, while in the shower he spots a huge, yellowish white spot on his glans. He goes to the doctor who recommends abstinence for a prudent period of between four months to a year, some injections, and an ointment. He's at home, in the bathroom, applying the pomade; the phone rings. It's a call from the insurance company: after a careful assessment they have decided the car *is* a total write-off and that's why they'll give him eighty percent of its scrap value, a paltry sum that provides the down payment for a second-hand vehicle, which he will pay for via a monthly standing order over three years, and in which he has an accident two days later on the motorway. They admit him to the hospital, operate immediately, and amputate his right arm. The man who, as well as trying on his mother's bras in front of the wardrobe mirror, had his first girlfriend at the age of fifteen, sells his car for a ridiculously low figure in order to get the necessary money to buy a prosthesis. Once the car is sold and the requisite tests have been carried out, the money left is barely enough to pay for the necessary tests to decide which is the best orthopedic arm for him, an arm that then proves to be well beyond his economic means.

From that moment on, one thing rapidly follows another. When he returns to work, he finds they are laying off staff, as a result of the economic crisis that has been impacting for many years, but is now surfacing ever more clearly. They fire him; they assure him his termination is in no way related to the loss of his arm, but even so he (who would give his other arm for that to be true) perceives that they don't seem that convinced when they tell him. The man who had his first girlfriend at the age of fifteen tries to look on the bright side: for months he will receive unemployment benefits. He's not overjoyed because he will be able to slack off. He's overjoyed because it means he'll have the time necessary to rebuild his life.

He calls his wife. Now that he has the free time, he'd like to see more of his children, the girl and the littl'un, whom he's not given as much attention as he should. His daughter picks up the phone and says she doesn't want to see him ever again, that she hates him. The man who had his first girlfriend at the age of fifteen and his first paycheck at sixteen hangs up; a tear rolls down his cheek. He looks out of the window: a group of policemen are making a charge on a group of demonstrators.

The second time he goes to collect his unemployment check, they say it doesn't exist anymore. The political and economic situation doesn't allow such state handouts. The man who received his first paycheck at sixteen discovers he can't pay his rent and must leave his apartment. He lives on what people give him in the subway. He always chooses the most crowded carriages. He walks in and in a dignified manner takes off his beret (he managed to get one: it's vital) and declaims: "Ladies and gentlemen, I'm sorry to bother you for a moment. I'm a one-armed, married man with two children: a girl and a young boy. I just got out of prison and I'm begging you for charity so I don't have to steal again. If it's sad to have to beg, it's even sadder to be forced to steal what others have earned through a hard day's work. Anything helps, thank you." He holds out his beret and parades it in front of the passengers. Until one day he comes across one who is very moved, and who tells him about an association of invalids that sells lottery tickets. He's one of the main instigators and will take the necessary steps for him to join. That happens in the morning. He joins in the afternoon.

The man who received his first paycheck at sixteen is allocated a pitch on a street corner, past which many cars drive though there are few pedestrians. That's why he ingeniously (like some fast-food restaurants that serve customers without them having to leave their cars) focuses his pitch on drivers and selling them tickets without them having to get out. Drivers stop near the curb and buy their tickets from behind the wheel. It's a huge success. He stands right on the edge of the curb, between two dumpsters, his lottery tickets attached to his shirt by clothespins. Cars drive close to him. Some stop. Some complain because the place where he stands means cars stop in a lane where they shouldn't. But as gas is suddenly rationed, there's much less traffic and none of the drivers are looking for an argument.

Soon there is no traffic; only tanks. The man who, as well as having his first girlfriend at the age of fifteen and his first paycheck at sixteen, never finished a masters in Business Studies, perseveres on his corner, full of hope, until a tank driven by a soldier fond of practical jokes flattens it. Now the man who didn't finish his masters is livid, but common sense leads him to decide to hide that when he finds out (from a woman running down the street close to the wall) that war broke out at half-past eight that morning. War!

As he is one-armed, they don't draft him. He is now really dead broke, eats edible leftovers he finds in trashcans in the city's posh upper reaches (if he's lucky and nobody in the same situation has beaten him to it) and sleeps in subway entrances. It's hopeless to beg in the subway now, because everybody is in the same state and nobody gives a thing. Months go by as if they were years and one day (almost backing up those who say the darkest moments always come before dawn) the war ends. As usual, the others win, and they, of course, occupy the city and impose new routines. The man who never finished his masters in Business Studies and, who, to boot, regularly played foosball for three years with his work colleagues, is pleased. The war is at an end and, no matter who has won, that's the best news possible.

However, many of his fellow citizens are not of the same mind. Previously, they say, at least there was the hope the war would finish someday. Now, as it is over, they don't even have that hope. Despair is so widespread that suicides abound. Men throw themselves off the terraces and balconies of their houses, wearing suits and hats. Mothers holding their children by the hand throw themselves under the wheels of trains and trams. Old folk choose to gas themselves to death. The timorous tie a big stone around their necks and hurl themselves into the sea. School students stick their fingers into power outlets and try to electrocute themselves. The man who regularly played foosball for three years with his work colleagues suffers ever more deeply whenever he trips over a suicide's body or sees a balcony window open and someone throw himself over. If he could, he'd run to save them . . . But the bodies fall so fast and by the time he gets there they have smashed against the ground. If only he could tell them that it's all about not becoming disillusioned or allowing oneself to be overcome by adversity . . . If one faces up to misfortune, the wind will always blow favorably.

Consequently, when the man who, as well as regularly playing foosball with his work colleagues for three years, always skipped the newspaper pages devoted to the economy, finds he has a chance to stop a suicide, he doesn't hesitate for a moment. As on dozens of occasions, he hears people scream when someone throws himself (or herself) or is about to throw himself (or herself) from a window. But this time the window isn't far away, but belongs to the same building by the side of which he keeps his belongings in a cardboard box. He looks skywards and sees a woman leaping from the sill of a window on the twenty-seventh floor. Without pausing to think he calculates the path of the fall and stands underneath, his arms (left arm and right stump, that is) open to catch her. As a result of the impact, the man who used to skip the pages devoted to the economy is flattened against the ground, like a blood-stained piece of gum. The woman, who has been saved against her own wishes, curses him and, in a frenzy of anger and frustration, kicks the corpse, which causes the immortal soul of the man who, as well as skipping the pages devoted to the economy, before he married spent two or three thousand pessetes every week on lottery tickets, hurriedly departs his mortal form and takes to the air, crosses the layer of cirrocumulus covering the city, crosses the stratosphere, the ionosphere, and the exosphere, reaches outer space, leaves the solar system and galaxy, comes to a halt several light years beyond, and dodges meteorites while he seeks in vain for a place to rest.

HALF-TWELVISH

THE MAN RELEASES A PUFF OF SMOKE AND PICKS UP THE telephone.

"Yes?"

"Hi." It's a woman's voice. "It's me."

The man's back stiffens. He squashes his cigarette into the ashtray next to the receiver. He speaks quietly: "I've told you a thousand times never to call me at home."

"But . . ."

"I told you, always call me at the office."

"Can you talk now?"

"Of course I can't. You know how it is."

"Where is . . . she?"

"In the bedroom."

"Can she hear you . . . us?"

"No, but she might walk in at any moment."

"Sorry. I'm really sorry. But I just had to call you. It couldn't wait till tomorrow, when you're at work."

There's a pause. It's the man who ends it.

"Why?"

"Because this situation is making me suffer endlessly."

"Which situation?"

"Ours. What else would I mean?"

"But . . . Let's see if we can get this . . . "

"No! No! Don't say a word. You don't have to." She tries to be ironic, but it doesn't come off. "She might hear you."

"No, she can't hear me now. Listen . . ."

"I think it's time we decided."

"Decided what?"

"Can't you guess?"

"I'm not in the mood for guessing games, Maria."

"I have to choose. Between you and him."

"And?"

"And, since you can't give me everything I want . . . Let's not kid ourselves: in your book, I'll never be more than a . . ." She takes a deep breath. The sound of an ambulance driving by in the distance is audible. "You don't want to leave her, do you? I don't know why I bother to ask. I know the answer."

"What's all that noise?"

"I'm calling from a pay phone."

"We've talked about this a thousand times. I've always been upfront with you. Open about things. You and I get along, don't we? So . . ."

"I really, really like you. But you know that's not how you feel about me."

"I've always said I don't want to hurt you. I never promised you anything. Did I ever make any promises?"

"No."

"You have to decide what we should do."

"Yes."

"Haven't I always said you have to be the one who decides?"

"Yes. That's why I called. Because I've come to a decision."

"I've always been honest with you." He stops. "What have you decided?"

"I've decided to . . . stop seeing you."

She says that and bursts into tears. She cries for a good long time. Gradually, her sobbing abates. He takes the opportunity to say something.

"I'm very sorry, but if that's really what . . ."

She interrupts: "Don't you understand, I *don't* want to *stop* seeing you?!"

When he can no longer hear her crying, he says: "Maria . . ."

"No." She sniffles. "I'd rather you said nothing."

He suddenly raises his voice: "You know, I'd go for a more economical car."

"What?"

"Especially if you have to drive so many miles." He stops for a second. "Yes, I see that. As far as that goes, I wouldn't know what to advise. But I think you should go for a car with a lot more . . . a lot more . . ." he acts as if he was looking for a word. "Okay, sure. But it's a gas guzzler."

"Can't you talk?"

"Obviously not."

"Is she close by?"

"Yes."

"In front of you?"

"Yes. But that model's more or less the same price as the Japanese one. And the Japanese . . ."

"Your wife's standing in front of you and I'm here, not knowing what I should do." She sounds increasingly indignant. "Not deciding once and for all to put an end to this misery."

"A four-door is ideal. For you guys, a four-door."

"You see, there's no alternative. We can't go on like this. We can't even have a civilized conversation."

"But that one uses a gallon and a half."

"You're talking about cars, gallons of gas, whether a four-door . . . and I can't even decide whether to hang up."

"Wait a second." He's covered the receiver with his hand. She can hear a muffled conversation. "He's saying . . ." He puts his hand back over the receiver. He removes his hand again. "Tell Lluïsa, from Anna, that her cake was perfect."

"Who does she think you're talking to?"

"Anyway, see you soon."

"Do you want me to hang up or . . . ? But before I do, tell me if we're meeting up tomorrow."

"Yes."

"I'm hopeless. I call you to say it's all over and end up asking you if tomorrow . . . Usual place?"

"Yes."

"Usual time?"

"Absolutely."

"And," she now speaks in honeyed tones, "will we do the usual? I'm imagining you on your knees, in front of me, pulling my skirt up . . . Will you lick me? Will you bite me? Will you hurt me really badly?"

"Yesss!" He suddenly lowers his voice again. "Fuck, Maria! She almost noticed. She's in the kitchen now, but she could be back any second. And what if she'd asked to talk to you?"

"But why would she want to?"

"I don't mean you: I mean the person she thought I was speaking to."

"Nobody gets you. And nobody gets me either. I don't even get myself. I obsess, I decide to end it, and, the second I hear your voice, all my good resolutions melt away. I really want to be with you now. Come to me. You can't? Course you can't. No matter. I get stressed when I can't talk to you. Do you love me?"

"Of course I do."

"I should hang up. Goodbye."

"Where are you?"

"In a bar, I told you."

"No, you said you were at a pay phone."

"If you knew already, why did you ask?"

"But you're not at a pay phone, you're in a bar. At least, that's what you're saying now."

"A bar, a pay phone, it's all the same."

"Oh, 'it's all the same. It's all the same.'"

"Hey, that's enough!"

"What are you going to do now?"

"Now? You mean about us?"

"No, I mean right now. Are you going to go see a movie? Have you eaten lunch? Do you have to go to your acting class?"

"Hey, I'm hanging up."

"Wait a minute."

"The fact is . . ."

"Maria, sometimes, I think, if we only wanted, if we only really tried, we'd make all this work differently, without all the tension."

"I expect we could."

"We could, so then . . .?"

"We could."

"What's the matter? Can't you talk? Is someone there, so that means you can't talk?"

"Hmm . . . Yes."

"You agreed to meet him in a bar and he's arrived. Or he was with you and now he's come over to the phone? Yes or no? What the hell . . . ?"

"I'll return the book. Don't you worry, my dear."

"Now you're addressing me as a woman."

"So, goodbye. Call me. And remind me to give that book back."

"Hey! Don't hang up! You made me suffer, listening to you, when I could only give fake replies and now . . ."

"I don't know that one. What did you say the title was?"

"Perfect. You're performance is terrific. Now you'll say what the book's title is. Or maybe you won't?"

"Right . . ."

"I really like that 'right.' It makes the conversation with that girl seem realistic, I mean, the girl one imagines you're talking to."

"*Love in the Afternoon,* did you say?"

"Is that title a come on?"

"But *The Hundred Crosses* was much better than *Love in the Afternoon*. At least as far as I was concerned."

"Hey, I haven't read that one either. Is it another novel?"

"*The Hundred Crosses* is boring?"

Suddenly he goes all serious again: "Hey, I told you. It uses much less gas than the other one."

"But the heroine of *Love in the Afternoon* is much more realistic."

"How is it a company like Peugeot didn't anticipate something like that?"

"But that was in *We're All Equal Now*. Right?"

"Absolutely."

"So then?"

"No, nothing."

There's a short pause.

"Do you see how impossible it is? I can talk again." There's another pause. "You there? Have you run out of steam, or do you want to change your automobile chat to something else?"

"I'm alone again."

"So goodbye."

"You're right. We should say goodbye."

"I have to tell you something first."

"Go on then."

"I'm pregnant." He doesn't respond. "Do you hear me? I'm pregnant. It's yours."

"What do you mean 'yours'? How can you be sure?"

"Because I've only done it with you since I had my last period, you idiot!"

"And what about this boyfriend who can give you everything I can't? Won't he . . . Sorry. What are you going to do?"

"What am *I* going to do? Doesn't this involve you in any way?"

"Not at all."

"Right. Now I see you for what you really are. Now I realize that, if I ever do find myself in that situation, you'd wash your hands completely."

"What do you mean 'if I ever do find myself in that situation'?"

"Obviously I mean I'm not pregnant. Do you think I'm stupid, or what? I suddenly thought of it, just to see how you'd react. Do you really think if I were actually pregnant I'd have asked for your opinion?"

His tone is angry: "You listen to me, Maria . . . !"

She retaliates: "What? Listen to what?"

"You know I won't be spoken to like that, in that tone, or have you try to put me down!"

"Oh, you don't say?"

"I'll wipe that smirk off your face!"

"Oh will you?"

"I'll knock you around."

"Yes . . ."

"Until you scream."

"Yes . . ."

"I'll tie you to the bedposts."

"Yes please . . ."

"I'll spit in your mouth."

"Yes!"

"I'll slap your face till blood flows."

"Yes please!"

"And I'll make you . . ."

"Do what? Make me do what?"

"I'll make you . . ."

"Do what?"

"I'll shove it in your mouth. I'll make you swallow it all: not a single drop will spill."

"Not a single one."

She's panting excitedly. He's really aroused.

"I said 'not a single drop.' Lick that one that's trailing down your lower lip."

"'Pig', call me 'pig' . . ."

"Pig. Get on your knees, and open your mouth."

She gasps.

"That's enough. I had to tell you no matter what. It's ridiculous to try to keep this up any longer." She goes quiet for a moment, as if preparing to launch back in. "Listen carefully: I'm not Maria."

"What do you mean 'I'm not Maria'?"

"I'm not Maria: that's what I meant. Maria is . . . Maria asked me to call you and pretend I was her."

"You're pulling my leg."

"She had to go somewhere. And wanted me to . . ."

"Where'd she go?"

"Out of town. She wanted you to think she was here and not . . . The fact is . . . I can't keep pretending. You know, Maria and I met in our drama class. I also study at the Theater Institute. She asked me to call you and get us to argue. Because you should be meeting tomorrow, but she won't be back. Do you hear me?"

"Where is she?"

"She's gone for a week. With a boyfriend."

"With who?"

"With Jaume."

"With Jaume?"

"Yes."

"Which Jaume?"

"Jaume Ibarra."

"Wait a minute: I'm Jaume Ibarra. Who did you think you were talking to? Which number did you call?"

"You're Jaume?"

"Yes."

"Fuck!"

"Who did you think you were talking to?"

"Joan."

"Joan? So you mean Maria and Joan are . . ."

"I get it now: I dialed that number, not the other one."

"And how come you've got my number?"

"Maria jotted down both numbers, one right above the other, and I picked the wrong one: I dialed one instead of the other."

"But why did she give you my number if you weren't supposed to call me? Or were you supposed to? But you just said you thought she'd taken off with me . . ."

"You wouldn't believe it if I'd told you."

"Tell me something, er . . . Who are you?"

"Carme."

"Carme, tell me some . . ."

She interrupts.

"Wait a moment. Are you really Jaume? Jaume lives by himself! Joan's the one who has a wife! Why did you say your wife was there with you?"

"Well, you're not exactly truth personified."

"If you thought you were talking to Maria, why did you make

me believe you had a wife?"

"The truth is Maria and I sometimes—not often of late, for sure, but sometimes—we do this kind of thing. It's a kind of game."

"She never told me."

"Why would she? Does she tell you everything?"

"Almost."

"Oh really? So what does she say about me?"

"Ooh."

"What does 'ooh' mean?"

"It means she tells me the interesting stuff."

"All the juicy details?"

"All the juicy details, and then some."

"Where are you?"

"I told you: in a bar."

"You told me you were at a pay phone."

"Not that again!"

"What are you doing now?"

"You asked me that already."

"When you were Maria. You're Carme now. Maybe you had something else to do. Besides, when you were Maria, you didn't answer me either." He bites his lip. "Why don't we meet up?"

"When?"

"Today?"

"It'll have to be tonight. I've got a class at five."

"Tonight then."

"Where?"

"In the bar at the Ritz?"

"Sure."

"At eight."

"My class finishes at eight. Make it half past."

"How will I recognize you?"

"I'll be wearing a fur jacket, the one you gave her a month before . . . I'll wear the fur jacket."

"A month before what?" She doesn't respond. "The jacket: I gave it to her a month before what?"

"I have to tell you, Jaume. Or I'm going to explode."

"Go on then."

"Maria's dead. You gave her that jacket a month before she died. You know . . . Listen . . . I shouldn't have . . . She . . . I know how much you loved each other. And when she died, I decided, all of us in the class decided . . ."

"I think this joke is in extremely poor taste."

"Let's meet and talk it over. At half past eight. Right? Or, if you want, I'll skip my class."

"I saw her last week."

"She's been dead five months."

"I've seen her lots of times over the last five months. I was with her last week. And she was very lively and very pretty. She was no ghost."

"For the last five months you've been going out with a Maria who wasn't Maria."

"And, according to you, who's been Maria all this time?"

"Me."

"I'd have noticed."

"I'm telling you the truth."

"If you were, why would you decide you don't want to come to our date tomorrow?"

"I'm fed up with pretending to be Maria."

"On the other hand, you just agreed to meet."

"Because I'll come as Carme, not as Maria. Please, Jaume, I'll explain later."

"So why didn't you realize I was Jaume and not Joan?"

"Do you think I didn't know who I was calling? Obviously you're Jaume. I know you perfectly. You've been my boyfriend for five months. And you learn a lot in five months. Even to the point that I . . ." her voice breaks, "I've fallen in love with you like a fool. And I want to put an end to this farce."

"I don't believe a word of this. How could you have managed it so I didn't notice you weren't Maria whenever we met up? Whenever, according to you, we met up."

"Well, I *am* studying acting."

"Even if you study acting! How could I not have noticed the difference? All I need now is for you to start in on a story of a twin sister . . . Hey, hang on: Maria has—had—a twin sister."

"Yours truly."

"I never met her."

"Oh, yes, you did. I mean, you have, and so often! Twice a week for the last five months. Sometimes only once a week. In fact, we need to talk about that. I want to see you more often. So, see you when we said? At half past eight?"

"Is your name really Carme?"

"At half-past eight, right?

"Yes."

"I love you so much. If you ever stopped loving me, I'd die."

THE URGE FOR SELF-IMPROVEMENT

DOROTHY SITS IN FRONT OF HER DRESSING TABLE. SHE SLOWLY runs her comb through her hair, while in the mirror she watches Tintin half-heartedly take off his jersey, half-heartedly throw it on to the sofa, and run his hand up through his beard, equally half-heartedly, and go to the shower. Dorothy stands up, takes off her dressing gown, puts it on the stool, gets into bed, and listens to the water splashing down. She thinks about picking up the book she was reading yesterday and reading for a while, but really doesn't feel like it. Better leave it where it was on her night table and wait for her husband to come out of the shower. She and Tintin could chat for a while. When Tintin comes back, still drying himself, Dorothy can see he's tired and thinks no way will he want to chat. She asks him if he's tired. Tintin says he is, gets into bed, says goodnight, puts out the light and, seven seconds later (while Dorothy gazes at him wondering whether to switch off her light too or, going back to her previous idea, to read for a while) he produces his first snore.

For some time it hasn't been like it was at the beginning. When did they last screw? Dorothy stretches the skin on her arm. It's saggy. She strokes her breasts. They droop. She's never had big breasts, but at least they used to be firm. Perhaps that's why. Her friend Carlota says these things often happen. She pulls back the sheet, gets up, switches off the light on her night table, and goes into the living room. She lights a cigarette and, while she blows smoke rings (she learned how to do that from her first boyfriend when she was seventeen), she looks at her reflection in pajamas in the balcony window. She runs her hand over her face. She has never thought of herself as beautiful. Those thin lips . . . The eyebrows that are too thick . . . The pointed nose . . . How can she expect Tintin to desire her? When you're young, soft skin and warm flesh make up for average looks. When you're past forty, things change.

That's why she decides to go to the beautician. She's going in the morning. She'll take care of her eyebrows. She spends the whole morning there and is delighted with the result. She looks at herself in a shoe-shop window. The moment she sees her, her friend Carlota says: her face is much improved by the reduced eyebrows, especially now that there are two. She arrives home feeling a mixture of hope and fear. Hoping Tintin will take one look, will find her incredibly beautiful, and they'll be as in love as when they started. And fearing he'll take one look, won't like the change, and will reproach her for being cheap and tawdry. Or, worse still, he'll laugh at her.

But Tintin comes home and doesn't even notice. A week later Dorothy goes to a cosmetic surgeon. She tells him she doesn't like her lips: they're thin, cold, and unattractive. He injects silicone. Her lips become full, sensual and voluptuous. Carlota says it's an amazing change and asks whether she's planning any others. Even though her friend was so positive, the experience over her eyebrows means Dorothy goes home with very little in the way of expectation. She's wrong: this time Tintin notices immediately. After months on hold, they copulate.

Reassured by her success, Dorothy goes back to the surgeon. She gets silicone breast implants. They look terrific. Firm, pert, and an ideal size. On this occasion, Carlota turns her nose up. She wonders whether she's not going too far, whether it all means to an extent she's no longer herself and is changing into a plastic woman, like the ones you see in films or in the magazines men buy. Does she still feel like herself despite the eyebrows, the swollen lips, and silicone breasts? Doesn't she feel a bit like an android?

Dorothy takes offence: of course she is still herself. Who else, if not? She concludes that perhaps it's simply that Carlota is beginning to envy her improvements. Dorothy goes back to the surgeon. At this stage in their professional relationship, there exists what one might call complete trust. That's why it is the surgeon who suggests the next step should be her nose. Dorothy wonders whether she shouldn't be annoyed at the way he's suggesting her nose is horrible; but she thinks it through: it would be stupid to take offence. The doctor is right; she knows that, and knows he's only saying that for her own good. She has it redone. Her little turned up nose arouses the lascivious in Tintin, wildly.

But right after they've shagged he looks at her suspiciously: "Who's prompting all the changes? Who are you out to please with your new lips, breasts, and nose? Don't lie to me, Dorothy." Dorothy rests her head on the marital biceps. I'm not doing it for anyone, she says. Only for him, although he thinks she's lying. And after she says that, she starts fantasizing. Perhaps now, with the new face and luscious breasts, she can dazzle all the men she wants. But is that what she wants?

It isn't. She simply wants to be ever-more appealing to her husband. That's why she immediately gets a facelift. And then gets hip replacements. That's on her surgeon's recommendation. It's a new technique that would have been unimaginable a few years ago, that allows you to replace broad, old hips with news ones constructed from semi-organic material. That means goodbye forever to cellulite and liposuctions. Before that, however, she has changes made to her legs (really gets the slenderest), and to her arms, arteries, and neck. The success of all these changes is confirmed one day when she's leaving the clinic and sees Carlota go in, stop at the reception and ask for an appointment. Despite all her warnings against, she's finally visiting the surgeon! At this point, Dorothy has changed so much she can enjoy watching Carlota without her recognizing who she is.

The next day, Dorothy goes back to the clinic. To make her cheekbones sleeker they alter her skull, and she doesn't feel quite herself for a few days. Particularly because of the small integrated circuit that, once inserted between the two hemispheres of her brain, allows her to scan all around her, see in the dark, and X-ray the insides of other people. When the bandages are removed, she goes for a walk down the corridor. Doctors, patients, and visitors look her up and down. If they only knew that her legs are prefabricated, her hips made from semi-organic material, and her eyebrows and cheekbones have been modified, if they only knew she has even had a small integrated circuit inserted, thanks to which she can read on the small screen of their eyes every one of their obscene thoughts when they look at her. Tintin isn't aware of that either; which is why, when he visits her that night at the clinic (later than he said), coming out with a silly excuse to justify his lateness, Dorothy discovers on the small screen of his eyes that it had been very hard for Tintin to decide, but finally, that night (hence his lateness) he told Carlota it's over between them. Dorothy hugs her husband and weeps tears of joy.

THE HIPPOCRATIC OATH

THE HEARTLESS MAN HAS TO WORK HARD TO GET HIS FRIEND TO drink himself silly so he can use the excuse of taking him home to sleep it off, in order to stay and listen to his wife complaining she is fed up with her drunkard of a husband. The heartless man listens, understands, and finally invites her to have a drink that turns into a binge. Until he gets her to drink herself silly, and they are in bed and she's saying she wants to leave her husband. That's when, all of a sudden, the heartless man's liver shatters: into ten thousand little pieces that splatter the wall, the ceiling, the sheets, and the tipsy lady whom he is about to rape and who half resists and repeats: "Why are you doing this to me? Why are you doing this?" She hasn't even noticed that the man's liver has burst and is all over his body. Horrified, the heartless man gets up, afraid he's going to collapse. He walks toward the bathroom. He looks in the mirror at the hole under his ribs on the right side of his body. There's a huge, dark breach where his liver once was. So the moment has finally come that, year after year, (from when he was sixteen, to be precise) the prophets in white coats have been forecasting. Their predictions are at last being fulfilled and the decades devoted to alcohol are producing the expected devastation.

Death, then, is imminent. Any moment now he will lose consciousness and fall to the ground. Nobody can really survive with such a hole in their side. Indeed, it's strange he hasn't yet dropped to the floor. How can he still be alive? How can he still reason? How can the rest of his body function without reacting, as if nothing has happened? He's just lost one of his indispensable organs and is alive, in the bathroom, and terrified. Perhaps because though it is indispensable, it's not the most indispensable organ. Let's be clear: it's not his heart that has burst. You can be sure if it had been, he'd have died some time ago. It's obvious there are indispensable organs and ones that aren't completely so, meaning, in fact, they cease to be indispensable. His liver clearly falls into the category of indispensable organs that aren't entirely so, and that liver has now become part of the bedroom's décor. From where he now hears coming the drunken, delirious cries of the woman, who is no longer asking why he's doing that to her, but where is he: "Where are you? Why did you leave me?"

He returns to her side. If he has to die, no better way to die than violently. No sooner does he get down to it than she asks endlessly: "Why are you doing this to me?" When he's had his fill, the heartless man goes to the bathroom, has a lengthy piss, congratulates himself on the optimal state of his kidneys (of which he's always been proud), washes his face, returns to the bedroom, takes the woman by the scruff of her neck, lifts her up, sits her in a chair, changes the liver-splattered sheets for clean ones, and lies on the bed. A while later, the woman gets up and gropes her way toward the bed because she can't even open her eyes. She lies next to the man and asks him if he is Frederic.

Next morning the heartless man wakes up with the clearest of heads. What happened to the hangover he should have? He remembers his liver bursting and doesn't even have time to imagine it was all a dream because he immediately confirms it wasn't: he sticks his hand in the hole in his right side. It's wide, about the size of his palm, and bloody, but not as much as last night. He can easily touch his lower ribs. He wipes his hand on the bedspread and realizes the woman is asleep next to him. He rapes her again. This time she says: "Don't do that again. Please, don't."

The heartless man showers, dresses, and tells the woman to get dressed. As they go down the stairs, the woman pukes twice. The heartless man, on the other hand, is as fresh as a daisy. He puts her in the car; in case she's forgotten, he reminds her of the state in which her husband came home the previous night and drops her by a subway entrance. Then he goes into a bookshop and skims through books about liver diseases.

He gets to his bar earlier than usual. He orders his first drink, afraid it will pour out of the hole. It doesn't. The hole has healed in a quick but unsightly fashion. By the time his friends arrive, the heartless man has been drinking for hours. He drinks as much as he wants the whole night long and has none of the unpleasant feelings you get whenever you drink way over the odds. And in the morning, no hangover.

He always drinks as much as he wants, and never feels the slightest negative effects. He eventually concludes that the liver is a kind of alien element installed in human bodies. Contrary to what people say (that alcohol in excess is to blame for liver problems), it is the liver that's to blame for a drinker's problems. The only path worth following is to increase alcohol intake to the maximum, ignore the warnings from medical prophets, and wait, longingly, for your liver to burst. A burst liver is simply one more natural, logical step in human development, like the falling out of baby teeth, the first nightly wet dreams, the decalcification of bones, or menopause. What generally happens is that one day, terrified by the advice from medics, people give up, stop drinking, or reduce their intake. That's where they are mistaken: by drinking less they halt the process toward the desirable bursting of their livers, and live uneasily between their pain and their guilty consciences. The fact that his liver burst is something normal is attested by the way the hole has healed spontaneously, with no issues at all. Quite the opposite to what would have happened if he'd gone to a doctor who'd have extracted his liver in an artificial, surgical operation.

The heartless man watches his drunken friends drop night after night, one after the other. The day always comes when, worried stiff by their pain, they go to their doctors and follow their advice, to a man. Victims of their own livers, they reduce their alcohol intake. One night, the heartless man advises them to drink much more, more and more, until their livers burst. If they do that, alcohol will never again be a problem. All the doctors know that's true, but they've made a pact to keep it quiet. His friends don't believe him, they drink a bit more and, totter home, drunk. He never repeats his advice. When they die of cirrhosis or hepatitis because they proved unable to rid themselves of their livers, he takes them a wreath, accompanies their widows to the funeral, and afterward, with the excuse that they need to drown their sorrows, he encourages them to drink to excess.

MYCOLOGY

As dawn breaks, the mushroom picker leaves home, with a stick and a basket. He walks along the road and, later, a path, until he reaches a pine grove. He stops now and then. He uses the stick to move away pine needles and find milk caps. He stoops, picks them, and puts them in his basket. Further on he finds penny buns. He continues walking and, in a clump of holm oaks, finds chanterelles, scarlet elf cups, portobello, and black trumpet mushrooms.

Once his basket is full, he retraces his steps. Suddenly he sees the rounded, white-flecked scarlet cap of a fly amanita. To ensure nobody picks it, he gives it a kick. A gnome appears in the midst of the dust cloud the mushroom creates in the air when it falls apart, a gnome with a green cap, white beard, and pointed boots with small bells on the toes, who stands half a yard tall.

"Good day, my good man. I am the lucky gnome who is born from some fly amanitas when they fall apart. You are a fortunate man, a lucky gnome is only found in every one hundred thousand amanitas. Make a wish and I will grant it."

The mushroom picker gives him a terrified glance.

"This only happens in stories."

"No," replies the gnome. "It also happens for real. Come on, make a wish and I'll grant it."

"I don't believe it."

"But you will. Make a wish and you will see how I'll grant you whatever you wish, even if it seems huge and quite beyond reach."

"How can I ask you for anything if I don't believe gnomes exist who can grant me whatever I ask for?"

"Here before you stands a little man with a white beard, green cap, boots with bells on the toes, half a yard tall, and you don't believe it? Come on, make a wish."

He could never have imagined himself in a situation like this. What should he ask for? Wealth? Women? Good health? Happiness? The gnome reads his thoughts.

"Ask for tangible things. Nothing airy-fairy. If you want wealth, ask for an amount of gold, or a palace, or a company with specific features. If you want women, say which ones in particular. If what you ask for makes you happy, at the end of the day, that's down to you."

The mushroom picker hesitates. Tangible things? A Range Rover? A mansion? A yacht? An airline? Kelly McGillis? Debora Caprioglio? The throne of a country in the Balkans? The gnome frowns impatiently.

"I can't wait forever. I didn't mention it before because I didn't think you'd take so long, but you have five minutes to decide. You've used three already."

So he's only got two left. The mushroom picker begins

to worry. He must decide what he wants and must decide straightaway.

"I want . . ."

He said "I want" though he has yet to decide what to ask for, simply so the gnome doesn't feel exasperated.

"What do want? Out with it."

"It's madness choosing in a rush like this. When you have an opportunity like this, perhaps once in a lifetime, you need time to decide. You can't ask for the first thing that comes to mind."

"You've got a minute and a half."

Perhaps, rather than things, it would be better to ask for money: an actual figure. A thousand billion pessetes, for example. He could have everything he wanted with a thousand billion pessetes. But why not say a thousand or a hundred thousand billion? Or a trillion. He can't decide on any figure because, in fact, in a situation like this, so charged with magic, he thinks it banal, trite, hardly subtle to ask for money.

"One minute."

As time is passing so quickly, he's unable to think coolly. It's unfair. What if he asked for power?

"Thirty-three seconds."

The quicker time passes, the harder it is to decide.

"Fifteen seconds."

A trillion then? Or a million trillions? Or a trillion trillions?"

"Four seconds."

He rejects outright the idea of money. An exceptional wish like this should be more sophisticated, more intelligent.

"Two seconds. Make it."

"I want another gnome like you."

His time is up. The gnome vanishes into the air and immediately, thud, another gnome appears in exactly the same place, exactly the same as the previous one. For a moment, the mushroom picker wonders whether it is the same gnome or not, but it can't be, because he repeats the same patter as the other, and if he were the same one, he thinks, he'd spare himself the bother: "Good day, my good man. I am the lucky gnome who is born from some fly amanitas when they fall apart. You are a fortunate man. A lucky gnome is only found in every hundred thousand amanitas. Make a wish and I'll grant it."

The second five minutes to decide what he wants have started to slip by. He knows, that if that's not enough, he can always ask for a gnome like this one, but that doesn't lessen his stress.

THE TOAD

THE ONLY BLUE ITEM WORN BY THE PRINCE ARE HIS (SKIN-TIGHT) pants, that define his buttocks, his firm, narrow buttocks that make all the girls and pederasts look twice and bite their lower lips when he walks by. He's also wearing a colorful doublet, a short, red cape, a gray, broad-brimmed hat with a green feather, and knee-length boots over his blue, skin-tight trousers.

He likes horse riding. He often mounts at dawn, after breakfast, and disappears into the woods that are dense, damp, and coniferous with a low mist. From time to time, in the middle of an esplanade, at the top of a hill, or next to a fir a hundred times taller than himself, the prince likes to rein in his horse, which whinnies, and he begins to ponder.

What is the prince pondering? He's pondering what he will do in the future, when he inherits the kingdom, how he will govern, the innovations he will introduce and the woman he will choose to sit by his side on the throne. The throne in that kingdom is a two-seater, upholstered in crimson velvet and very similar to a sofa or a chaise longue. It's not that he must marry to inherit the kingdom. His grandfather, for example, inherited it as a bachelor, and continued to be a bachelor for the first eight years of his reign until he met a well-balanced, worthy princess, the prince's grandmother. So he doesn't have to, but he wants to resolve the issue so he can dedicate himself entirely to governing immediately after his coronation.

But it's hard for him to find a woman who is worthy and well-balanced. He rarely goes out. Princes like him, his friends, go out every night, crawling from tavern to tavern and party to party, until the early hours, sometimes not hiding their princely state and sometimes disguised as plebeians. They get bored of meeting princesses and plebs in parties and taverns. At noon every day, after getting up, the princes meet up for an aperitif, red eyes hidden behind shades, heads like lead. They discuss in minute detail the woman or women they did the previous night and how they did them. They always reach the same conclusion: it doesn't matter whether they are princesses or plebs; they're all bitches. This concession to egalitarianism is so unusual and is greeted with guffaws by everyone. Except for the prince in blue pants. The prince doesn't like them frivolously comparing princesses and plebs, or declaring that there isn't a single woman who isn't a bitch.

That's why he never goes out with the other princes, who, to convince him, say he should go out with them one night. If he agreed, he'd see that things are as they say. He refuses. He doesn't refuse because he doesn't believe them. He refuses because he is afraid to accompany them and discover that, in effect, they are right. And he is convinced that, if he doesn't lose heart, he is going to find the pristine princess he's been seeking since puberty. Conversely, if he reaches the conclusion that, aristocrats or plebs, they are all the same, he will never find her.

He has never confessed to anyone how he hopes to find his ideal princess. Because he knows they would laugh at him. He will find her in an enchanted state: in the form of a toad. He is convinced of that. It's precisely why she will be different from all the others, because she'll have remained far from the banality and degradation of humans. He's read that in stories, from a very early age, and, even though the other princes (the same who now meet at noon every day for an aperitif) make fun of those stories, he really believes them. And it is a belief reinforced over the years by a strange, symptomatic circumstance: he has never succeeded in finding a toad. From a very early age he has eagerly sought them out. He knows what they look like from drawings and photographs in natural science books, but he's never found one.

Consequently, on the morning when, after galloping for hours, he stops near a pool so his horse can drink and he sees a toad on a mossy rock (a greenish-purple, fat, shiny toad), he dismounts, heart beating a hundred times a minute. Finally he has found a toad, face-to-face, for real. The toad greets him: "Croak."

It's a much more disgusting animal than he had imagined from the drawings and photos in his books. But he doesn't doubt for an instant that it is the animal he must kiss. It is the first toad he has succeeded in seeing after years of looking, and that's why he knows it is no ordinary toad, but an enchanted princess, who has not been led astray by mundane life. He ties his horse's reins to a poplar and advances fearfully. Fear of the disappointment he will feel, even though he's dead sure, if it turns out that the toad is only a toad and takes a leap into the pool. He kneels down by the rock.

"Croak," goes the toad a second time.

The prince bends over and moves his face forward. The toad is right in front of him. Its belly inflates and deflates, nonstop. Now he can see it so close-up he's filled with loathing, but he casts that aside immediately and brings his lips nearer to the toad's mug: "Smack."

For less than a thousandth of a second, to a deafening din, the toad changes into a prism of a hundred thousand colors, that multiply their facets infinitely until all the colors and faces transform into a beautiful girl with golden tresses. Topped by a crown that proves her noble lineage. The prince has finally found the woman he has always sought, the one with whom he will share his life and his throne.

"You finally came," she says. "If you only knew how long I've waited for the prince who was to release me from the spell."

"That prince is me. I've been looking for you ever since I was a little boy. And I always knew I'd find you."

They look into each other's eyes, and hold hands. It is forever, and they both know.

"It was as if this moment was never going to come," she says.

"Well, now it has."

"Yes."

"That's great, right?"

"Are you happy?"

"Yes. What about you?"

"I am too."

The prince looks at his watch. What else can he tell her? What should they talk about? Should he suggest they go straight to his place or will she take it the wrong way? They really are in no hurry. They have their whole lives before them.

"Well . . ."

"Yes."

"You see . . ."

"So much waiting and, all of a sudden, bang, it's done."

"Yes. It's done."

THE SLEEPING BEAUTY

THE KNIGHT SEES THE GIRL'S BODY IN THE MIDDLE OF A CLEARING, she's sleeping on a bed made of oak branches and wrapped in flowers of every color. He quickly dismounts and kneels by her side. He takes her hand. It's cold. Her face is white, as if she were dead. And her lips are thin and purple. Conscious of his role in the story, the knight kisses her sweetly. The girl immediately opens her eyes, big, dark, almond eyes, and looks at him: with a surprised look that straightaway (when she has weighed up who she is, where she is, why she is there, and who that man by her side must be and who, she imagines, must have kissed her) is tinged with tenderness. Her lips lose their purple hue and, when they've recovered the redness of life, they open out into a smile. Her teeth are very beautiful. The knight has no regrets about having to marry her, as tradition stipulates. What's more, he can already see himself arm in arm with her, sharing everything, having first a boy, then a girl, and finally another boy. They will live a happy life and grow old together.

The girl's cheeks have lost their deathly pallor and are already pink, sensual, ready to be kissed. He stands up and holds out his hands so she can take them and pull herself up. And then, while (always looking lovingly into his eyes) the girl (weak from spending so much time prostrate) stands up thanks to his strong male arms, the knight notices (twenty or thirty yards further on, long before the clearing gives way to the woods) another girl asleep, as beautiful as the one he's just woken up, lying like her on a bed of oak branches and wrapped in flowers of every color.

THE MONARCHY

All thanks to that shoe she lost when she had to run from the ball because the spell ended at midnight, her dress turned back into rags, her carriage ceased to be a carriage and turned back into a pumpkin, the horse into mice, etc., she has always been astonished that the shoe only fitted her perfectly, because her foot (a size 36) wasn't at all out of the ordinary and other girls in town must have worn the same size. She still remembers the shocked expressions on her stepsisters' faces when they saw she was the one marrying the prince and (a few years later when the king and queen died) became the new queen.

The king was an attentive, passionate husband. It was a dream life until the day she found a blotch of lipstick on the regal shirt. The earth gave way under her feet. How disappointing! How should she react, a woman who has always behaved honestly, unmaliciously, who is virtue personified?

It's obvious the king has a lover. A blotch of lipstick on a shirt has always been obvious proof of adultery. Who can her husband's lover be? Should she tell him she has found out or should she pretend she hasn't, as she knows that is a queen's traditional response, in such cases, in order not to endanger the institution of the monarchy? And why has the king resorted to a lover?

Doesn't she leave him properly satisfied? Maybe it's because she refuses practices she believes to be perverse (sodomy and golden showers, basically) that her husband now seeks elsewhere?

She decides to say nothing. She also says nothing the day the king only reaches the royal bedchamber at 8 A.M., with big rings under his eyes and smelling of women. (Where do they meet? In a hotel, in her house, or even in the palace? There are so many rooms in the palace, he could easily allow himself to have his lover in any of those rooms she doesn't know about.) Nor does she say anything when the carnal contact they once enjoyed with the regularity of a metronome (tonight yes, tomorrow no) becomes so infrequent that one day she realizes it's been two months since the last time.

Every night she cries silently in the royal bedroom, because the king no longer goes to bed with her on any night. Loneliness makes her angry. She'd have preferred never to have gone to that ball, or for some other girl's foot to have fitted that shoe before hers. Thus, after accomplishing his task, the prince's envoy would never have come to their house. And, if he had ever come, she'd even have preferred one of her stepsisters to have worn a size 36, instead of a 40 and 41, sizes that were too big for a girl. Then, the envoy wouldn't have posed the question that now, feeling devastated by her husband's infidelity, she judges to have been ill-omened: whether any other girl lived in the house, apart from her step-mother and step-sisters.

What's the point of being queen if the king doesn't love her? She'd give everything to be the woman the king was laying extramaritally. She'd a thousand times prefer to be at the center of the monarch's nights of adulterous love than to lie in the empty, conjugal bed. Better mistress than queen.

A former servant, she decides to follow tradition and not tell the king what she has learned. She'll act stealthily. The following night, when the king courteously says goodbye after dinner, she follows him at a distance. She follows him along passageways she doesn't know, through unfamiliar wings of the palace, to rooms she didn't even imagine existed. The king walks ahead of her with a torch. Finally he enters a room, shuts the door, and she is left in the passage, in the dark. She immediately hears voices from inside. Her husband's, for sure. And a woman cackling. But above that laughter she hears another woman's voice. Does he have two in there? Gradually, trying not to make a noise, she opens the door a crack. She stretches out on the floor so they can't see her from the bed; she slips half her body inside. The light from the candelabra projects the shadows of three copulating bodies onto the walls. She'd have liked to lift herself up to see who's in the bed, because she can't identify the women from their laughter and whispers. From where she is stretched out on the floor, she can see barely anything; she can only see, thrown haphazardly at the foot of the bed, her husband's shoes and two pairs of extremely high-heeled women's shoes, one black, size 40, and the other red, size 41.

THE FAUNA

THE CAT CHASES THE MOUSE AROUND THE HOUSE AND KEEPS falling into the traps he himself sets for the rodent. He falls into a pot of tar, slips on a banana skin, and runs into a meat mincer that chops him into tiny pieces. When he's still groggy, he touches the door handle not realizing the mouse has connected it to an electric current: his hair stands on end, he turns from black to white, to yellow, to purple, his eyes leap out of their sockets and spin round eighteen times, his zigzagging tongue lashes in and out; singed, he drops to the floor and turns into a heap of steaming black dust. Until his mistress comes with a brush and pan, sweeps him up, and tips him into the trashcan.

But he's immediately back on the alert. Oh! He'd give his all to be rid of that wretched mouse, which shouldn't arouse anyone's sympathy. Why does he never win out? Why does that little beast always escape? What's more, the cat knows that most of humanity loathes mice. What most people remember in horror from the ups and downs of war, are not dumdum bullets, sleepless nights and starving days, or trekking unshod with their feet wrapped in rags, but the rats. Why then do some humans forget their loathing and come out on the side of mice? Is it simply because they are the tiniest of creatures?

The cat returns to the charge. He swears yet again that the mouse won't escape this time. He burns the house down; everything goes up in smoke, though the mouse survives. And when the master gets back from work, he beats the cat with a broom. The cat doesn't relent. He chases the mouse yet again. Finally he catches it, throws it into a cement mixer, is about to switch it on, when the dog appears. As the result of a law that is as incomprehensible as it is atavistic, the dog is always a friend to the mouse. That dog is carrying a humongous hammer in one paw. He brings it down on the cat's head, flattening it like a sheet of paper.

But he revives straight away, receives a parcel in the mail and smiles. He fills the den where the mouse is hiding with gunpowder and puts a match to it. Everything explodes, but he has enough time to see that the mouse wasn't inside and is now smirking repulsively at him from the front doorstep. Nothing ever changes.

Until many episodes later, the astonishing day comes when the cat is victorious.

After a chase down the hallway in the house (a chase like so many others), the cat catches the mouse. That has happened so often, but . . . The cat has held the mouse in his fist so often, like now, that not even the cat can believe this time he's onto a winner. He spikes the mouse on a three-pronged fork, and blood spurts from each of the three wounds. The cat lights the burner. Puts a frying pan on top. Pours in oil. When the oil begins to spit, he throws in the mouse, which gradually fries, squeaking so frenziedly even the cat pops a cork into both of his ears. That's when he begins to understand that on this occasion something strange is happening. This time it is for real. The mouse's body stiffens, turns blacker and blacker, and gives off smoke. The mouse stares at the cat with a look the cat will never forget, and dies. The cat continues to fry the corpse. Then he removes it from the frying pan and burns it straight on the flames until it's reduced to black, furrowed skin. He takes this from the flames, scrutinizes it closely, and touches it with his claws: the skin crumbles into a thousand incinerated flakes that the blustery wind scatters to the four points of the compass. For a moment the cat feels hugely happy.

STRENGTH OF WILL

THE STUBBORN MAN KNOWS THAT IT'S ONLY A MATTER OF HAVING (and sustaining for whatever time is necessary) the firmness of will to achieve his goal. There are no other factors or unknown quantities. He kneels down, lowers his torso until his face is a few inches from the stone (a rather elongated, smoothly rounded, gray stone), and vocalizes clearly: "Pa."

He stares at the stone for a while, focusing his eyes on every irregularity, trying to take it all in, to establish total communication, until the stone becomes an extension of himself, a few inches away. It's high noon; the breeze makes up for the sun's brightness. He re-opens his lips sparingly: "Pa."

He chose "pa" because he'd always been told that it's the first thing children say, the burst of sound that surprises parents, the easiest syllable with which to start speaking.

"Pa."

The stone is still silent. The stubborn man smiles. He doesn't yield easily to adversity. He decided to teach the stone to speak knowing it would be no easy task. He knows that, over the centuries, humanity has thought little of the verbal potential of the mineral kingdom, which means that, perhaps for the first time in many a year, a sober man is cheek by jowl with a stone, trying to make it speak. If we add to that the traditional idleness of learners, the difficulty of the enterprise is self-evident.

"Pa," persists the stubborn man.

The stone is quiet. The man throws his head back for a moment, then immediately brings his face in close, some five inches from the stone: "Pa pa pa pa pa pa. Pa!"

No response. The man smiles again, strokes his chin, straightens his torso, stands up, takes a cigarette packet from his pocket, extracts a cigarette, and lights it. He smokes while he contemplates the rock. How can he establish contact? How can he communicate with it? He uses his fingers to flick the cigarette against a tree, and (like a wrestler to his opponent) sways over the stone shouting: "PAAA!"

The stone's apparent indifference endears him. He caresses it with his fingertips. Now he tries to speak seductively: "Stone. Hello, stone. Stone? Sto-one. S t o n e. Stone . . ."

He caresses it nonstop. First slowly, then quickly. First gently, then frantically.

"Come on, say it: pa."

The stone says nothing. The stubborn man gives it a kiss.

"I know you can, I don't know if you're listening, but I know you understand. Do you understand? Do you get me? I know you can say it. I know you can say 'pa.' I know you can speak, if only a very little. I also know you find it difficult, because maybe nobody has ever spoken to you or asked you to speak to them, and these things are an effort, initially, if you're not accustomed.

I'm aware of all that. That's why I'm understanding; I'm not asking you to do anything you can't do by making a minimal effort. Now I'll repeat it again. And, you, right away, will repeat it with me. Agreed? Hey, come on. It isn't easy, but it's not impossible either. Come on, say it: pa. Pa. Pa."

He places his ear up against the surface of the stone, to see if the efforts it is making translate into a whisper. But they don't: silence. Total silence. The stubborn man breathes in deeply and returns to the charge. He gives the stone new arguments, he tells it why it must be such an effort to speak and what it must do to succeed. When night falls, he takes it in his hands and wipes off the earth stuck underneath. He takes the stone home. He puts it on the dining-room table, ensures it's comfortable. He lets it rest the whole night. The next morning he wishes it a good day, washes it carefully, under the stream of water from the tap, with lukewarm water: not too cold, not too hot. Then takes it out on to his balcony. From the balcony you can see the whole valley, summer vacationers' chalets scattered around, one end of the lake, and, in the distance, the lights from the highway. He leaves the stone on the table and sits on a chair.

"Come on, say it: pa."

Three days later the stubborn man makes it clear that he is angry: "Very well, don't speak. Don't think I haven't registered your tacit contempt. You don't need to say anything to make your contempt obvious. I'll only say one thing: nobody makes fun of me."

The stubborn man takes the stone in his right hand, squeezes it (so much so his face turns a bright red), and finally hurls it energetically. The stone describes an arc in the sky: over the valley, over the chalets and swimming pools of the summer holiday-makers, over the man pushing the lawn mower, over the road being repaired, over the highway with little traffic, over the industrial development area, over the soccer field where a team in green shirts and white shorts and another in yellow shirts and blue shorts are tied, over the buildings in the provincial city, until it falls right in the middle of a square, at the feet of German tourists who are so focused on photographing the cathedral they don't notice the stone fall, crash against the paving stones, and, as it breaks, emit a sharp sound quite like "pa!"

PHYSIOGNOMIES

THE EGGHEAD IS INCAPABLE OF REMEMBERING A SINGLE FACE. When he meets someone who says hello in the street, he never knows who he is or why he knows him. Maybe the odd face rings a bell, but he never manages to assign a name, or work out where he made their acquaintance. He has become so expert at avoiding the stressful scenes his poor recall inevitably creates, that (so people don't notice he doesn't know them) he says hello to whoever says hello to him. So impassively and so naturally that nobody realizes he in fact doesn't recognize them. He's even capable of sustaining conversations on general (and not so general) topics and, when they finally say goodbye, with a pat on the back or a handshake, the stranger walks off convinced the egghead hasn't doubted who he was for a moment. Above all, you must show huge pleasure from the start. So the other person doesn't have time to formulate doubts. Immediately he sees he's been recognized, he exclaims loudly: "How are you? How's life treating you?" There's nothing worse than to seem at a loss, or say hello in hushed tones, because the stranger would eye him suspiciously and ask the fateful question: "You don't remember me, do you?" A question you can't answer with a lie, because it means it's quite obvious the person questioned doesn't have the slightest clue about the individual standing in front of him.

He has never remembered a face. Not even as a child. At school he deduced who the teacher was because he was taller and bigger than other people in the classroom. And he couldn't identify his classmates, as they were all smallish (more or less his height). Each had a different face; how could they expect him to remember them all and know which belonged to whom? Fortunately, at home he knew his father was his father because he was the tall, grown-up person in the house. And, although he shaved daily, he felt his beard, especially when he kissed him. His mother, on the other hand, didn't have a beard, and her skin was very soft. She generally wore a skirt, which meant it was even easier to recognize her. Perhaps that was why, when she wore trousers, he could feel disconcerted for a moment, until he honed in on her slender hands and soft cheeks. He easily identified his brother: he was the other boy, the other shorty in the house. If there'd been more adults or siblings, he'd have started to have problems. And the same happened every morning when he looked at himself in the mirror and saw a face he didn't recognize. Obviously, it was his, but if it had been among five others, he wouldn't have recognized it.

Consequently he is astonished years later when he goes into the subway by his house and sees a girl coming out and recognizes her. They aren't at all acquainted and they've never spoken, but he remembers precisely that he saw her, only for a second, thirty-eight years ago, on the day he went to collect his degree certificate. She was leaving the office, wearing a blue cardigan, white blouse, and gray skirt.

For the first time in his life he has recognized a face, a face he has only seen once, many years ago. He is stunned. (Should he have reconsidered? Should he have turned round, followed the woman, and told her he has remembered her from years back, from a day when she was leaving the faculty office? It would have made no sense. Most likely the young woman would have seen it as a cheap ploy to accost her and would have ignored him.) He can't get over it: the only face he has recognized to this point, from throughout his life, is precisely the face of woman he'd only seen once thirty-eight years ago. This, he deduces, should indicate something about his own personality, his way of being, the reasons for the lack of physiognomy indicators that has accompanied him through life. He is convinced this riddle must contain the key to what gives meaning to his life—a successful life but one marked implacably by his inability to remember a single face. It can be no chance thing that the only time he saw that woman again he'd not found it at all difficult to remember and pinpoint her. Nevertheless, however much he ruminates, he can't discern any key. Days, weeks, years pass by. He remains unable to remember any face for the rest of his life. He often ruminates on that. She demonstrates he *is* able to remember a face; he definitely remembered her, that time when he saw her coming out of the subway, he thinks, full of hope; blissfully unaware she's always lived in the same street as him (precisely two houses from his) and that he has seen her hundreds of times, before and after that day when he recognized her in the subway.

DIVINE PROVIDENCE

One morning, the scholar who in a patient, disciplined manner has dedicated fifty of his sixty-eight years to writing the Great Work (of which he has currently completed seventy-two volumes) notices that the ink of the letters on the first pages of the first volume is beginning to fade. The black is no longer so distinct and is turning grayish. As he has become used to frequently revisiting all the volumes he has written to date, when he notices the deterioration, only the first two pages have been affected, the first that he wrote fifty years ago. And, into the bargain, the letters on the bottom lines of the second page are also rather illegible. He painstakingly restores the erased letters one by one. He diligently follows their traces until he has restored words, lines and paragraphs with Indian ink. But just as he is finishing, he notices that the words on the last lines of page 2 and the whole of page 3 (when he began the restoration process, some were in a good state and others were in a relatively good state) have also faded. Confirmation that the disease is degenerative.

Fifty years ago when the scholar decided to devote his life to writing his Great Work, he was already well aware he would have to dispense with any activity that might consume even a tiny fraction of his time, remain celibate, and live without a television. The Great Work would be really so Great he wouldn't be able to waste a moment on anything else. Indeed there could be nothing else *but* the Great Work. That was why he decided not to waste precious minutes looking for a publisher. The future would find one. He was so convinced of the value of what he was setting out to do, that, of necessity, when somebody discovered the volumes of the Great Work, unpublished, side by side, on the book case in the hallway in his house, the first publisher to discover it (whoever that might be) would immediately recognize the importance of what was before him. But, if letters are now fading, whatever will remain of his Great Work?

The degeneration is relentless. Just when he has re-worked the first three pages, he finds that the letters on pages 4, 5, and 6 are also fading. When he has re-worked the letters on pages 4, 5, and 6, he discovers those on 7, 8, 9, and 10 have been erased completely. When he has re-worked 7, 8, 9, and 10, he finds those on page 11 to 27 have vanished.

He can't waste time trying to deduce why the letters are being erased. He concentrates on re-working the first volume (the first volumes: he soon sees the second and third volumes are also deteriorating) and realizes that the time spent doing that won't allow him to finish the concluding volumes. Without the colophon that should give the volumes he has already written their true meaning, his fifty years of dedication will have been for naught. The initial volumes are simply the necessary, though not essential, groundwork to situate things in the space where he must set out his genuinely innovative findings: namely, the final volumes. Without the latter, the Great Work will never be that. Hence his doubt: shouldn't he perhaps let the early volumes continue to fade and not waste time restoring them? Wouldn't it be better to focus on his struggle against time to finish once and for all the final volumes (exactly how many are there: six, or seven?) so he can bring the Work to its climax, even at the risk of the first volumes fading away forever? Of the seventy-two he has written so far, he can certainly afford to lose the first seven or eight; even though they enabled him to gather a head of steam, they don't contribute anything substantially new. However, then another doubt strikes him: when he has written the final full stop, will only the first seven or eight volumes have faded? Determined not to waste one minute more, he buckles down to it. Then immediately stops. How come he hasn't realized until now that, if he dies, and that person fated to discover the Great Work and take it to a publisher dilly-dallies in making the discovery, the afflicted volumes won't be seven or eight but the whole lot? What should he do: stop writing and start seeking out a publisher right now, to avoid that risk, even though, without the concluding volumes, it will be impossible to demonstrate that his project is genuinely ground-breaking? However, if he devotes time and effort to looking for a publisher, he won't be able to dedicate the necessary time to re-working the volumes as they keep wasting away, nor will he be able to write the final volumes. What should he do? He becomes a nervous wreck. Could a life of endless toil have been in vain? Yes, it could. What *was* the point of so much effort, single-minded devotion, celibacy, and sacrifice? He thinks it has been one huge practical joke. He feels hatred growing within himself: hatred toward himself for a life misspent. And his inability to recover the time he has wasted doesn't panic him as much as being certain that at this juncture it will be too late to decide how to make the most of the time that remains.

THE STORY

In the middle of the afternoon the man sits at his desk, takes a sheet of paper, sticks it in his typewriter, and starts writing. The first sentence comes to him immediately. The second too. Between the second and the third he hesitates for a few seconds.

He fills a page, extracts the sheet from the carriage, and puts it to one side, blank side up. He adds another sheet to the first, then another. Now and then he rereads what he writes, crosses out words, changes the word order within sentences, eliminates paragraphs, throws entire pages into the trash. He suddenly pushes his typewriter back, grabs the heap of completed pages, puts it in front of him, and with a ballpoint crosses out, changes, adds, eliminates. He places the heap of corrected sheets to his right, returns to the typewriter, and rewrites the story from top to bottom. Finally, he corrects it manually again and rewrites on the typewriter. Well into the night he reads it for the nth time. It's a story. He really likes it. So much so he weeps tears of joy. He is happy. It may be the best story he has ever written. He finds it to be nigh on perfect. Nigh on, because it lacks a title. When he finds a suitable title, it will be the best story possible. He wonders what to put. One comes to mind. He writes it on a sheet of paper, to see what he thinks. It doesn't entirely work. Indeed, it doesn't work at all. He crosses it out. He thinks up another. When he rereads it, he crosses it out too.

All the titles that occur to him ruin his story: either they are obvious or else give the story a surrealist edge that destroys its simplicity. Or else they are crass and spoil it. For a moment, he thinks of putting *Untitled,* but that appalls him even more. He also seriously contemplates the possibility of not giving it a title, and leaving the space he's left for it blank. But that solution is the worst possible: perhaps the odd story doesn't need a title, but not that one; it needs just the right one: the title that would mean it ceased to be an almost perfect story to become the altogether perfect story: the best that has ever been written.

By dawn he gives up: there is no title that is sufficiently perfect for that story that's so perfect, no title good enough, which prevents it from being altogether perfect. Resigned (and knowing it is all he can do) he takes the sheets where he has written the story, rips them down the middle, rips those halves down the middle; and continues ripping until he has reduced them to shreds.

Quim Monzó was born in Barcelona in 1952. He has been awarded the National Award, the City of Barcelona Award, the Prudenci Bertrana Prize, the El Temps Award, the Lletra d'Or Prize for the best book of the year, and the Catalan Writers' Award, and he has been awarded *Serra d'Or* magazine's prestigious Critics' Award four times. He has also translated numerous authors into Catalan, including Truman Capote, J. D. Salinger, and Ernest Hemingway.

PETER BUSH is an award-winning translator from Catalan, French, Spanish, and Portuguese. His translations from the Catalan include Juan Goytisolo's *Níjar Country,* Teresa Solana's *A Shortcut to Paradise,* Alain Badiou's *In Praise of Love,* and Josep Pla's *The Gray Notebook.*

OPEN
LETTER

Elsa Morante (Italy)
Aracoeli
Giulio Mozzi (Italy)
This Is the Garden
Andrés Neuman (Spain)
The Things We Don't Do
Jóanes Nielsen (Faroe Islands)
The Brahmadells
Madame Nielsen (Denmark)
The Endless Summer
Henrik Nordbrandt (Denmark)
When We Leave Each Other
Asta Olivia Nordenhof (Denmark)
The Easiness and the Loneliness
Wojciech Nowicki (Poland)
Salki
Bragi Ólafsson (Iceland)
The Ambassador
Narrator
The Pets
Kristín Ómarsdóttir (Iceland)
Children in Reindeer Woods
Sigrún Pálsdóttir (Iceland)
History. A Mess.
Diego Trelles Paz (ed.) (World)
The Future Is Not Ours
Ilja Leonard Pfeijffer (Netherlands)
Rupert: A Confession
Jerzy Pilch (Poland)
The Mighty Angel
My First Suicide
A Thousand Peaceful Cities
Rein Raud (Estonia)
The Brother
João Reis (Portugal)
The Translator's Bride
Mercè Rodoreda (Catalonia)
Camellia Street
Death in Spring
The Selected Stories of Mercè Rodoreda
War, So Much War
Milen Ruskov (Bulgaria)
Thrown into Nature
Guillermo Saccomanno (Argentina)
77
Gesell Dome
Juan José Saer (Argentina)
The Clouds
La Grande
The One Before
Scars
The Sixty-Five Years of Washington
Olga Sedakova (Russia)
In Praise of Poetry
Mikhail Shishkin (Russia)
Maidenhair
Sölvi Björn Sigurðsson (Iceland)
The Last Days of My Mother
Maria José Silveira (Brazil)
Her Mother's Mother's Mother and Her Daughters
Andrzej Sosnowski (Poland)
Lodgings
Albena Stambolova (Bulgaria)
Everything Happens as It Does
Benjamin Stein (Germany)
The Canvas
Georgi Tenev (Bulgaria)
Party Headquarters
Dubravka Ugresic (Europe)
American Fictionary
Europe in Sepia
Fox
Karaoke Culture
Nobody's Home
Ludvík Vaculík (Czech Republic)
The Guinea Pigs
Jorge Volpi (Mexico)
Season of Ash
Antoine Volodine (France)
Bardo or Not Bardo
Post-Exoticism in Ten Lessons, Lesson Eleven
Radiant Terminus
Eliot Weinberger (ed.) (World)
Elsewhere
Ingrid Winterbach (South Africa)
The Book of Happenstance
The Elusive Moth
To Hell with Cronjé
Ror Wolf (Germany)
Two or Three Years Later
Words Without Borders (ed.) (World)
The Wall in My Head
Xiao Hong (China)
Ma Bo'le's Second Life
Alejandro Zambra (Chile)
The Private Lives of Trees